THE VIGILANTE'S LOVER

VOL. 2

Annie Winters
Tony West

www.anniewinters.com
www.tonywestwrites.com

casey shay press

Casey Shay Press
PO Box 160116
Austin, TX 78716
www.caseyshaypress.com

ISBN: 9781938150388

Also available in digital format.
eISBN: 9781938150371

Library of Congress Control Number: 2015931046

FIRST EDITION

Also by Annie Winters

Writing as JJ Knight
The UNCAGED LOVE Series
The FIGHT FOR HER Series

Writing as Deanna Roy
Forever Innocent
Forever Loved
Forever Sheltered

Learn about appearances and events at
www.deannaroy.com

For all the fans who are part of
ANNIE'S VIGILANTES!

You all seriously rock.

1

Mia

Jax's face pulses red with the alarms going off inside his car.

An automated female voice announces, "Ten seconds until security breach."

I kiss him one more time. This is my only shot at convincing him to keep me. Even if his enemies have us surrounded, I can't let him forget that.

His lips are unhurried, as if we're not in the middle of a disaster. The calm car voice starts counting down how long we have until we're caught.

I break the kiss. Jax stares past me out the windshield. Thinking.

I'm straddling him in the driver's seat, my skirt hiked up to my waist. I'm a little shocked at my own behavior, but desperate times call for desperate measures.

My neck tingles. But I don't think about it for long because Jax's fingers brush my skin there. No wonder I'm feeling so many sensations.

The driver's door is wide open. I can't see whatever the car's security says is coming, but I believe it. The technology in this thing is like nothing I've ever seen before.

We've escaped the Vigilante stronghold only to be caught by them again. I'm pretty sure they'll be more careful with us the second time.

Jax reaches out and closes the door. Then he presses a button on the dash. The motor roars to life. "You might want to hang on," he says.

My wet sweater dress clings to me, cold and heavy. I'm not sure what I should hold on to in this position. I shift as if I'm going to switch over to the passenger seat, but then we abruptly shoot forward, and I fall into Jax.

I'm not going to be able to move now. I flatten

my cheek against his chest so he can see around me. My arms snake behind him to wrap around his back.

Bushes and small trees crunch beneath our tires. We swerve to the right, then the left, a dizzying zigzag. Jax is a Vigilante, part of a powerful underground network of spies and law enforcement. He is skilled, and his car is powerful, but the people coming for us are just as good.

I bury my face in his wet shirt. We had to jump in a river earlier to escape detection by our heat signatures. Whatever we're doing, I don't want to look. The last thing he needs is my silly screams distracting him.

I hear a strange sound and look up to see a panel in the roof sliding open.

"Watch out for the console," Jax says.

I turn my head toward the inside of the car. Between the two front seats, the padded black leather armrest opens. I pull my elbow in tighter as a silver canister rises up from it.

"It's going to shoot out," he says.

The word "Crybaby" is scrawled on the side as if someone has written on it with a marker.

Suddenly the canister rockets up and out the rooftop. Even though I was warned, I have to stifle a yelp of surprise.

Jax's arms move around me as he steers, powerful and strong. I steal a glance out the side window. The trees are less dense. I don't see anyone following us, but the red alarm is still going off. Then the car voice says, "Threat retreating."

We bump onto a regular road and the ride is smoother. My knees are killing me in this position, but I don't know if I should move to my seat. The rooftop closes and the console snaps shut.

The red light inside the car stops pulsing. I can feel Jax relax beneath me.

"What was that thing that just shot out of your car?" I ask.

"Long story," he says.

"I have time." The more we talk, the more sure I feel that he won't dump me on the side of the road like he had planned.

"All right. Sam has a thing for that old television show *Firefly*," Jax says. "He makes lots of custom modifications to our cars based on things they used in the episodes."

"I don't know that show," I say.

"It's about space cowboys," he says. "They were always getting into scrapes."

"What does the Crybaby do?"

"In the show it makes a fake distress call," Jax says. "But Sam's Crybaby actually jettisons our car identification, so they follow it instead of us."

"Your Vigilante friends seem easy to fool," I say.

"The person fooling them is a Vigilante himself," Jax says. He shifts in the seat, adjusting my position on his lap. "The best there is."

"Will I get to meet him?" I ask. I hold my breath for the answer.

"Not unless you want to cost him his job," he says.

That told me nothing. I decide it's probably time to move to my side, even though I don't want to. I lunge clumsily over to the other seat.

"You feeling all right?" Jax asks.

"A little cold, maybe." Truth be told, I might be a little nauseated from his crazy driving. But I'm not going to tell him that. If I complain the littlest bit, he might ditch me.

I glance down, grimacing at my pale legs sticking out of the wet red dress, ending in the once-white, now-muddy shoes. I pull the skirt down, embarrassed now at how I hiked it up to straddle Jax and keep him from leaving me in the woods.

"So this Sam person who made the Crybaby, is he the one who gave you the case of tech tools?" I ask.

He glances over at me. "You have a good memory for details," he says.

I warm over with the compliment, then shiver. I'm starting to feel considerably worse. "Your car doesn't have a blow-dry setting, does it?"

It's not a serious question, but Jax taps a button on the dash.

"This will work," he says.

Hot air blows hard on my face. I turn my head, trying to get my hair less dripping wet. Our leap into a river means I look like a drowned rat.

Despite all its fancy tech, this car still has a normal pull-down visor, presumably with a mirror on the back side. I lower it to assess my appearance. Probably Jax isn't terribly attracted to wet, shivering, bad-haired women.

I'm surprised to see what appears to be an ordinary mirror compartment and light. I slide the panel to reveal the mirror, then blink as a green light scans my face.

"Female companion," a voice says, and dims

the bulb to a more flattering brightness.

I laugh. "Really? All your important getaway gadgets, and the only thing your mirror does is make me feel better about myself?"

"You might want to close that within thirty seconds," Jax says casually.

I snap my focus back to the mirror. I see a tiny red light blinking in the corner. Is it a weapon? Something to incapacitate a passenger? Or kill them?

My fingers fly to shove the panel back in place.

Jax laughs. "I was just kidding."

I hunker down in my seat. "I can't trust you for anything."

"Seeing as I tied you up before we even met properly, I'd say that is a fair assessment of our relationship."

I pull at the wet dress, still sticking to my skin. I'm not sure where we stand now. Jax finally seems to recognize that I'm not his enemy. His manner is light and easy compared to the rage he shot at me when he thought I'd killed his friend.

Like I could do anything like that.

I swallow hard, thinking of that searing kiss. But the sick feeling persists. I can't banish it even with those hot memories.

The dress is cloying, cold and clammy. My face feels flushed. “I want to change,” I say.

“We’re not in any imminent danger,” Jax says. “You can climb in the back.”

I crawl awkwardly between the seats. My head is pounding. Something in my neck tingles again. I press my hand to the spot, but it feels normal.

My butt lands awkwardly on the seat, squashing the bag with my other outfits. I try to sort through them and pull out the navy pants, but my vision seems to be failing. Everything is going black and white.

I manage to pull the dress up and over my head. The red bra and matching thong are also damp, but I’m not going to take those off. I glance up at Jax and catch his eyes on me in the rearview mirror. He doesn’t break his stare just because I see him looking. His riveting attention is unnerving.

I flush with heat again. I’m tempted to take the bra off after all, just to taunt him. My belly flutters at the thought of being so forward, so bold.

Then the sick feeling comes back full force. I manage to cry out, “Jax!” before everything goes totally dark.

2

Jax

Shit.

I'm watching Mia get undressed, that glorious body revealed again, when she suddenly passes clean out.

They got her. I suspected it.

I glance at the display on the dash. The majority of the Vigilantes are still clustered around the Crybaby, but several have strayed away. Two are following my path, out of luck or awareness of my position, I don't know.

Anything in this car could be tipping them off, and now I have a poisoned woman to deal with.

I saw the dart hit her neck when she was on my lap. I knew it was meant for me. I pulled it from her instantly, but apparently the injection system has improved during my time in Ridley Prison. There was no delay at all.

I have about seven minutes until it kills her.

I check the distance of the blips again, and scan the landscape for a safe location to pull off the road. It will do me no good to stop for the antidote if I immediately get stalled by Vigilantes. By the time I can fight or talk my way back to Mia, it will be too late.

I jerk the wheel to cut down a narrow driveway that looks like it might lead to a single residence. The density of the trees on either side of the path obscures whatever might be at the end of it.

Based on the condition of the fencing, the place is either abandoned or inhabited by elderly people who can no longer keep it up. All good things.

As soon as I'm out of sight of the road, I slam on the brakes and jump out the door and into the backseat.

Which poison is it? I press my fingers to Mia's

neck. Her breaths are slow and shallow, her pulse fluttery. Has to be respiratory, as the neurological one causes spasms.

I'm torn on what to do next. Dismantle anything Vigilante to avoid detection, or go straight for the vials of antidotes and try to figure out which one to try?

I check the display. The blips still show the Vigilantes' approach. Until they pass the drive I turned down, I won't know if they are on to me. I can't risk them coming. I still have five solid minutes for Mia.

I race to the front seat of the car, powering down all the transmitters, jerking open the glove compartment and pulling out the wires powering all the systems that were custom-fitted by Sam. I assume that even though I jettisoned the Crybaby and our identity chips, the Vigilantes scanned all the tech in the car when it was abandoned and can follow it.

That done, I race to the trunk and tear through everything in it. I power off every detector, all the security features, and then take apart anything with a power source.

Now we should be black, emitting nothing but

body heat signatures that aren't easily tracked by their moving vehicles. At the same time, without any tech, I won't know they're coming if they do. The entire system is down.

But never mind that. I have to go for the vials. I open the side compartment to the black valise Sam left for me. Inside are five syringes. I can't just use them all. The antidotes are as bad as the poisons themselves if I use the wrong one.

I think through them carefully, glad now that I took the time on the original drive to Mia's house to listen to Sam's rundown of the contents of the car. The blue vial is for the neurological dart, which I ruled out. The red one is a digestive one, a painful torture poison that would have made her sick before she passed out. Yellow is a snuff dart, which is rarely used. This vial isn't an antidote. It chemically alters the poison in their system to hide what you did. Mia would already be dead if they'd used this one.

The last two are powerful drugs meant to incapacitate prior to the kill. I don't believe for a minute they just sedated her. Vigilantes stationed on the perimeters of silos don't even carry anything that isn't lethal. The seven-minute time span means they can save you if they want to.

But which one? Green or white?

I snatch them both and head to the backseat. Dilated pupils. That will tell me. One of the poisons will affect your eyes. The other won't.

I lean in close to Mia and take her head in my hand. Her honey hair spills down, dark and wet from the river water. My throat is tight as I push on her eyelids to check her pupils. The blacks are normal sized inside her green irises.

I lay her down more comfortably on the seat and pick up the white vial. I'm sure that dart was probably meant for me. Whoever aimed the shot should be downgraded to floor-mopping duty. Vigilantes should never miss their target.

I tug the cap off the needle and stick Mia gently in the crook of her arm. When the syringe is empty, I recap it and look outside the car. If the Vigilantes are truly tracking me, they will arrive any second.

I wait, counting heartbeats, for either Mia to wake up or a car to bear down on us.

Neither happens.

I lay my head on Mia's chest, listening. Her heartbeat is less rapid, but her respiration is still slow, too slow. The dart contained more than her slender body could handle. The dose was meant for me.

Damn it. I peer up the driveway. There's a structure just visible around a bend. I pull an oversized shawl from Mia's clothing bag and cover her with it. Then I get back behind the wheel and slowly ease the car down the lane.

I assess my own emotional state as we move. I'm more anxious than I should be. I've lost my own cold control.

Calming breaths. Stay alert and prepared.

I'm vulnerable, I know, with all my tech disabled. But I just waltzed out of a Vigilante silo with nothing more than a universal passkey. I'm up for this.

It's the girl. She's setting off a buzz inside me that doesn't respond to my training. I want to protect her, keep her safe. And right now, I've failed at that.

We pull up in front of an old farmhouse. It's definitely abandoned, the front door hanging from its frame. I drive around behind it to hide the car. Farmland that has been encroached upon by brush and small trees stretches as far as I can see. To my left is a barn that looks like it is in good shape. I'll move the car in there once I know Mia is all right.

I kill the car and turn to check on her. Still out, but I'm reassured by the rise and fall of her chest beneath the shawl.

I debate leaving her in the car while I investigate the house and make it secure. But I can't do it. If the Vigilantes do wander down this drive, they'll take her. And if she has some unexpected reaction to the poison or the antidote, I want to be there.

The house is two stories. The back steps look solid. The open front door might actually be a suitable ruse, making the house look empty. I just need to secure one of the rooms.

I walk to the back of the car and lift Mia into my arms. The shawl falls away, revealing the creamy skin again. She shivers, which I take as an excellent sign. I tuck the shawl around her and pull her close.

One swift kick at the back door pops it open. The kitchen is dirty but intact. One exit leads to an empty dining room. Another goes to a hall and straight to the open front door. Not secure at all. I turn past the stairs to check and see if there is a bedroom downstairs, but there is only an empty room with a splintered wall piano and an old armchair losing its stuffing.

This is no good. I roll Mia into me and peer out the front window. Still no sign of anyone.

I return to the kitchen and out the back door. Mia starts to stir, taking in a sudden sharp breath. I pause by the car, looking down at her. Her eyelids flutter but don't open.

She's coming out of it.

I hurry toward the barn. There's a giant set of doors out front, but a normal-sized door on the side near the house. Instead of kicking it, I test to see if it will open without damaging it. I grimace when Mia's bare knee brushes the rough surface as I turn the knob.

The inside is dim, splinters of light coming in through the cracks. The building is cavernous, open, and strewn with hay bales. A rickety ladder leads up to a loft.

Much easier to defend.

I kick at a crumbling hay bale until it falls apart. It's not quite enough, so I knock a couple others around until I have a suitable pile.

The shawl slides off Mia easily, and I kneel to hold her in my lap as I spread it out on the loose hay. When I set her on it, she immediately curls into a tight ball, shivering. My shirt is pretty dry now, so I strip it off and cover her with it. It won't be enough, but it will have to do for a moment.

I pull the shawl around her and wait. Her pulse seems normal, and her respiration also seems to have settled. I'm not sure why she's not awake. I shake her lightly. "Mia, are you all right?"

Her face scrunches in pain.

I've only been poisoned once by a Vigilante dart, the torture one, on accident when Sam was testing one of his hidden injectors. He administered the antidote within seconds, but coming out of it was still an unsavory experience. I imagine Mia is not feeling too well at the moment.

I brush her hair off her face. Finally, her eyes open. "Jax?" she says.

"You were taken down by a medicated dart," I say, deciding to soften the seriousness of the hit. "You'll be fine in a moment, but you might feel a little sick."

She looks around. "Where are we?"

"A barn."

She coughs out half a laugh. "Back to my roots."

"You can take the girl out of the country," I say.

"But you can't take the country out of the girl," she finishes. Then she frowns. "Did you lose your shirt?"

"It looks better on you."

Mia glances down. "Oh," she says.

"I think you were changing when the dart took effect," I tell her.

She tugs the shirt more tightly around her. "I don't remember."

Her closeness now that she is awake starts to become a distraction. I'm still surprised by her unexpected kiss, tying me down. Yes, I definitely need to put some distance between us.

"I'm going to get your clothes from the car," I say and stand up.

"Are we safe here?" she asks.

"For a while. Until you recover a bit."

She sits up. "Where are we going?"

I was expecting this question. I'm not sure if I should continue to placate her, or tell her the truth.

But my hesitation gives me away. She struggles to her feet. "You can't take me back to Tennessee. I won't go!"

"Mia, you are acting like a petulant child."

"You weren't treating me like a child a few minutes ago!"

God, she's so difficult. Why won't she just let me get her to safety?

"If you stay with me, we're both dead," I say.

"You got us out of the silo. We jumped into a river! I kept up with you!" Her eyes flash like fire in the dim barn. The poison's definitely out of her system. Or the antidote is making her slightly manic.

"We work well together!" she insists.

She stands before me, clutching the shawl and my shirt. Her hair falls over her bare shoulders, the red straps of her bra bright against her skin.

I have to get some distance.

"I need to get some supplies from my car," I say.

She reaches out her hand. "I want to go out there with you."

Does she think I'm going to just leave her here in the barn? "I'm not going to desert you here," I tell her. "We're miles from anywhere."

"Can you just sit down for a minute?" she asks, tilting her head. Her green eyes are visible even in this light.

"In the last few hours, I've been interrogated, locked up, forced to climb a ladder in the pitch black, chased by strangers, and shot with a dart," she says. "You owe me a moment."

She plops back down on the hay, letting the shawl and my shirt fall into a puddle in her lap. Her bare shoulders lead to the red bra. It's not substantial at all, just sheer wisps that accentuate her puckered nipples in the chill.

"Sit down," she insists. Her voice has an edge to it, like a schoolteacher who expects instant obedience.

I hesitate. I want to secure the doors, pull some weapons, set up a defendable position. But my legs aren't involved in that decision, and I settle in the hay next to those enticing buds poking through fabric as thin as air.

I'll listen to what she has to say, if only to keep looking at her.

3

Mia

Huh. It worked. Jax sits next to me in the hay.

I'm not stupid. I dropped the shawl in my lap on purpose. I don't think I'm up for another lap wiggle, not with all the rejection handed to me on a platter in the last hour. But he's here.

His shirt is off. I haven't seen this much of him before. I've been at a disadvantage since I met him. He's been in those expensive suits, like he's headed to an office party, every minute of our time together.

Meanwhile I've been in shredded nightgowns,

ropes, or high heels I can't walk in.

Except now, in the barely there lingerie given to me by the women he hired.

My heart hammers, just looking at him. His chest is smooth and muscled. His arm muscles bulge, but not in a bodybuilder way. Just strong.

His belly is rippled, flat, and looks like planking is something he does in his sleep.

I want to keep him. I want him close. I know how he looked at me at the hotel. I know he wanted me then. I just have to figure out how to get back to that.

So I'm sitting in a cold barn on a pile of hay in a sheer bra and a thong. Time to go for broke.

"Do you have to take me home?" I ask.

"Mia. You know I have to."

At least he's admitting it. But I can't go back there. I have nothing. No one. And this life? Narrow escapes. Car chases. Danger. It fits me. I know it.

I tear my eyes from his bare chest to glance around the barn. I won't have much time to convince him that I am up for the task of being his sidekick. I rack my brain for something that will impress him.

Rope. There has to be some rope around here.

The red silk one is probably in the car still, but I can't let him go fetch it. He might change his mind about listening to me.

This is a barn. Rope is standard issue.

I spot a coil of it hanging on a hook near the main door. "I need you to teach me something," I tell him.

His eyes meet mine. There's not a lot of light in here, just the parts coming through the cracks, but I can see him well enough. He's wary. Maybe a little tired. "What do you need to know?"

I stand up and let the shawl and his shirt hit the ground. His gaze locks on my body. I realize he may have misunderstood, and a jolt of fear mixed with excitement zips through me. Before he can say or do anything, I walk over to the coil of rope.

I can feel him watching. The underwear leaves nothing to the imagination.

I have to work hard not to feel ridiculous. Imagine me, small-town Mia, prancing around in tiny red lingerie around someone like Jax.

He waits, silent, observant. I take the rope off the wall and sense his interest pick up, even though I can't see his expression from here.

I'm glad I'm not in the heels now. Tripping

over my own feet would not add to this moment. But I have the feeling that the Phase One training shoes might be just as sexy to someone like Jax. Doesn't matter. It's what I've got.

I walk back over to him. Sitting in the hay, his face hits the level of my thighs. I have a terrible urge to move in very close, but I don't know anything about that, how to keep him interested without looking silly.

I hold out the rope. "I want to know how you escaped my constrictor knot in the car."

He doesn't bother to pretend to look at anything but me. His eyes travel up my knees, thighs, and pause on the slender strings of the thong. The straps come together with a bit of sheer fabric that matches the bra and hides nothing, not the wisps of hair or the dark line he now seems fixated on.

I feel a rush of heat and a sudden wetness. But I'm used to it. I felt it from reading his letters. I'm not afraid anymore, although I guess I should be. I got on the shot in college, hoping for a love affair that never happened. So I'm not afraid that I'll end up pregnant. But I might fear that I'll like everything, love everything, need everything, and he'll leave anyway.

"So you want me to teach you how to escape a knot?" he asks.

"Yes."

"As if you're being trained?" he adds.

"Just like a Vigilante would," I say.

"Then get naked," he says.

"Wh-what?" I stumble over the question. What does that have to do with escape training?

His voice is calm and impassive. "A Vigilante doesn't question her training."

I hesitate. "If I do well, will you let me stay?"

"Get naked," he repeats.

It's a test. I won't fail it. I'm shy and a little embarrassed, but this is moving me in the direction I want to go. So I'll do it.

I kick off the shoes. The barn floor is rough and littered with loose hay. I lean down and set the coil of rope on the floor.

I reach behind me for the hook of the bra. I fumble for a moment and realize my hands are shaking. I don't know how far this is going to go, but I'm going to agree to anything Jax asks. This is my one shot at convincing him to keep me, and I'm not going to be afraid.

The straps slide down my arm, and I let the bra fall to the floor. I resist the urge to cover myself.

"Stand up straight," he orders.

I realize I'm hunching over, as if my shoulders could come forward and hide me. I lift my chin and let my arms dangle loosely at my sides. My chest comes out, the taut nipples out in front.

Jax leans back on his elbow in the hay. "Panties."

I stick my thumbs in the straps.

"Slowly," he adds.

I swallow past the lump in my throat. I ease the thong down my thighs. My hair is almost dry now and tickles my skin as I bend a little to push the panties past my knees. When they fall free, I stand tall again.

"Come closer," Jax says.

My heart hammers in my throat. I take a step toward him, close enough that he can reach up and touch me anywhere.

His hand wraps around my ankle and slides up my calf. I can't breathe, the sensuous feel of his palm against my skin is so intense.

He reaches my knee and keeps going, up my thigh. I can feel my pulse between my legs, and the hot wetness there, waiting for him. I've never been touched there by anyone, and the need for it is so great that I want to bend down and meet him halfway..

But without warning, he smacks the bend at the back of my knee. It drops me into the hay, right on the shawl I left a minute ago. In a flash, both my wrists are encircled and over my head, pinned by his iron grip. His naked chest brushes against my breasts and I'm so shocked by how quickly he got me down that I cry out.

"You want to learn to escape from this?" he asks.

"Yes," I say. "That's what I want."

His face is inches from mine. His eyes linger on my lips, and I wonder if he is thinking of kissing me again. I want him to, need him to. It's a fiery desperate longing I don't think I can contain. My chest heaves from my labored breaths, creating a friction where our skin touches.

"You made one constrictor and four slipknots in the car," he says. "That was your mistake." He glances up. "Let's lash you to something."

He reaches beneath me in the hay and scoots my body, shawl and all, closer to a post.

The rope hisses as he slips it around the rough wood. I can't see the knot he ties. I can't concentrate on that. His chest is so near, hot and bare. I want to touch it but I'm bound. I arch a little to reestablish our contact.

Jax sits back to study his knots. I look up. My hands are pressed tightly together, bound to the post. I can barely move them at all. I don't see any way to get out of this.

"The hardest part of escaping is staying focused," he says and picks up the frayed end of the rope. "I have a feeling this might be one of your weaknesses." He grabs my knees and jerks them apart.

I suck in my breath. I don't know what he's going to do next. The rope is in his hands and he lets it dangle until it brushes between my legs.

The contact is electrifying and I can't help it, but I cry out. I tug against the bonds. I want my hands.

"Think about the knots, Mia. You know how they are tied. You know how they go." He trails the end of the rope against my tender parts again.

I'm on fire. The withdrawal of the rope is painful and leaves me aching with desire. I want it harder. I want more. I want to ease this fiery need.

"Harder," I find myself whispering, a little shocked.

Jax pauses for a second, surprised, but he complies. The rope slaps against me with just a touch of sting. The contact is titillating, a burst of pure pleasure.

"More," I plead.

"Untie the knot," Jax says.

I try to move my hands, but they are bound tight against the post. My body heaves as I thrust my hips toward Jax. "I can't do it," I say. "Please."

"Distraction," he says as he examines the end of the rope. "You're failing."

I stare up at my hands. I can follow the turns, but I can't move at all to do anything about it.

The rope brushes my belly and I focus on Jax again.

"I should loosen these ends a bit more," he says. "It's a basic sisal three-strand. The beginnings of a nice flogger. Just what you're aching for."

I swallow hard as he unravels more of the strands. The hot pleasure is already retreating, and I want it back. He uses one loose piece to wrap the end so the rope won't come undone.

"Think about that overhand turn," he says. "And how you can reach it."

I can't concentrate on anything but my need of that powerful strike, and his eyes on me, full of lust and interest and surprise. He's pleased with me, and that is as powerful as the pleasure of the contact.

But he sits back. He won't do anything, give me any more, unless I impress him.

I jerk against the ropes. They are rough and chafe me quickly, unlike the smooth silk we used before. I keep pulling them apart, but then realize I have room to work if I instead clasp them together.

"Now you're getting it," Jax says. He's finished this handmade flogger. I'm rewarded for my progress with a sharp smack between my legs with the frayed ends of the rope.

This one has more force, but he knows it, and lays his hand against my skin to calm it.

I lose concentration again, my body lifting up against his palm.

"You like this?" he asks, and applies more pressure.

"Yes," I breathe. I'm on fire again, my body hot and throbbing.

"Untie it and you'll get a lot more," he says.

I clasp my hands together and stretch my finger. Yes, I can get it to the first knot. I poke into the knot like I'm holding a marlinspike tool to separate the strands. Any knot that can be tied can be undone. It's just a reverse puzzle.

My finger works inside.

"Very nice," Jax says.

I pause, waiting for the rewarding strike. This one has bite, aimed more precisely. I cry out, then drift into a long moan when his hand cools the burn. This time his thumb slides down, gently brushing against the swollen bud.

I lurch up again, pressing into his hand. I want so much more. I want everything.

But Jax retreats, slapping the end of the rope casually against his palm.

I work harder on the knot, releasing the first one. My arms drop about an inch, and I can reach the second far more easily.

"Mmmm," Jax says. "Nicely done." He drops the rope. This time he spreads my knees and slides both hands up my thighs. His thumbs press into me, splaying me so wide I feel a cool rush of air against the newly exposed folds.

I want more, to work this so fast that he

doesn't stop, that there is no pause. I slip my finger into the second knot and work it free. Just two more.

He doesn't release me, but keeps working, one thumb circling the sensitive bud, and the other slipping along the wet spaces that welcome him greedily.

Now that I have room to work, the last two knots are easy. I pull them apart, and my arms fall away from the pole.

"Escaping bonds is a mind game," Jax says. "Work with the knots, not against them."

I can't listen to anything. His fingers are making magic down below. I clutch his shoulders now that I'm free, and feel along his biceps. I haven't touched anyone like this. I want to. I want to explore all of him.

Jax leans over me, bracing on one arm. His finger slips a little more deeply inside. I arch up and into him.

Sparks are bursting through me. My sensations are heightened, the smell of hay, the soft fuzz of the shawl, Jax's breathing near my ear. He moves closer and his lips lock onto my breast, sucking lightly.

A buzz starts to build down low. I've never felt anything so intense. My need to be filled, to release the pressure, is maddening, unrelenting.

Jax's movements increase in speed, delving more deeply. But something makes him stop and lift his head, looking at me. I don't know what has happened, why he quit. My chest heaves.

He watches me quietly, concern on his brow, then he seems to shake it off. His fingers move back to the nub, and I close my eyes and the friction starts to reach something, to create some sort of synergy.

I relax into the hay and let it come over me, ripples like muscle contractions taking over my body in places I didn't know existed.

Then suddenly the pleasure blasts out like a shock wave. I can't stop myself from crying out, from saying Jax's name. It's too intense, too crazy, overwhelming and beautiful and wild.

I shudder around his hand. I can't breathe, can't talk, can't think as I start to come down. This is what people talk about. This is why people do crazy stuff. This.

I want more. So much more. I want it again and again. I clutch at Jax. "What did you just do?" I ask.

His face looks puzzled. "This is new to you, isn't it?"

I don't want to answer. I don't want him to know how inexperienced I am.

"I felt the resistance," he says.

This is not the sexy talk I expected. It's like an interrogation. I let go of him.

"Did you do the restructure surgery?" he says. "Were you in the program once?"

I bite back my disappointment even as my body still hums against his hand. I don't know what he's talking about. What restructure? What program?

Then it hits me. The hymen surgery. Fake virginity. Apparently it's something certain types of operatives do.

"I didn't even know people did that until you told me about it," I say. I don't know what he's getting at, why he stopped. Doesn't he want to do the rest? I sink into the hay. This feels over already. I want to weep.

Then I get it. He doesn't want to be with a virgin. Or to destroy an expensive surgery.

He withdraws his hand. I grab at it, stopping him from pulling away. "It's okay," I say quickly. "I don't mind doing this. With you."

His Adam's apple bobs. He looks genuinely

concerned, something new. "You've never done any training, then," he says.

"Do they take your virginity during it?" I ask, half sitting up. Surely not!

"Depends," he says.

"What?"

"Most girls come in after college. It's long gone."

I feel really naked now, too exposed for this conversation. I let go of him and cross my arms over my chest. "Well, mine isn't."

"I realize that."

"Is it a problem?"

The ground crunches outside and Jax leaps to his feet. Before I can even figure out what he's doing, he's snatched an axe from the wall and is crouching next to the door.

Which is opening.

And I'm naked and sprawled out in the hay.

I grab the shawl and drag it around me. Jax's shirt is near my feet so I pick that up too.

The door only opens an inch. A friendly voice says, "You got a woman in there, don't ya?"

Jax visibly relaxes, although he doesn't set down the axe.

"Who's with you?" he asks.

"Just Colette." The door opens wider and a broad dark-skinned man in a blue T-shirt and jeans appears in the gap.

Now the axe comes down. "How the hell did you find me?" Jax asks.

"We headed toward the silo the minute you stupidly set foot in it," Sam answers. "Then about an hour ago you powered down. Figured you'd only do that in a jam."

"You had it transmit a signal, I assume," Jax says.

"Indeedy." He looks around the barn until he spots me. "Yup, there's the woman." He calls out behind him, "I owe you a cheeseburger, Colette!"

"Vegetarian!" a voice calls back with an accent like women in perfume commercials, exotic, with an unexpected lilt. French, I guess.

"Jax, my man, you've lost your shirt!" He extends a hand.

Jax sets the axe on the ground and shakes the hand firmly. "Gave it to the lady," he says and nods his head at me.

I clutch the shawl around me, grateful that it is large, and try to give a little wave with my fingers.

“I’m Sam,” he says. He walks forward as if to shake hands, then realizes my situation, holding tight to the shawl. “Jax is terrible with introductions.”

“Mia,” I say.

His gaze falls to the Phase One Trainee uniform shoes on the ground.

“You snagged a Phase One?” he asks Jax and lets out a whistle. “Good thing their ID transmitters are short range.”

“Long story,” Jax says. “Is Colette coming? We have to find out who killed Klaus.”

“We wanted to talk to you about that. I’ll fetch her first.” Sam heads back out into the sunlight.

When he’s gone, Jax turns to me. “I guess you’ll want your clothes now.”

His reflexes are good, so he manages to dodge the clod of dirt I fling at his face.

4

Jax

This girl is something else.

Her eyes are wild as she lets a hunk of dirt fly at me. The effort causes her to lose her grip on the shawl and it glides back to the hay.

I sidestep so she misses but don't stop looking at her.

So luscious.

The light from the cracks in the barn makes bright stripes on her skin. I'm not sure which I like better, her standing there, angry as hell, or lying back, enjoying my attention.

"Yes, I want my clothes," she snaps.

I hold up my hands to fend off anything else she might throw at me. "I'll fetch them."

I'm still taken aback by her lack of experience. She's definitely not in the Vigilante program. Honest-to-God virginity is a bit of a liability in that game. Besides, the training alone tends to throw young people together in ways that just seem to encourage a lot of carnal acts.

But this Mia. I don't really know what to do with her.

Since I haven't left the barn yet, she snatches my shirt, still lying at her feet, and sticks her arms through. It's too large and ends about mid-thigh. I think she might look sexier in it than out of it, although perhaps that's because I imagine taking it off again.

It may be just as well Sam arrived. A situation like this takes some consideration. And time.

"Sometime this year, maybe?" Her voice spits fire. She probably didn't appreciate Sam's suggestion that I'm always with a woman. He's not very good at saying the right thing in front of ladies.

Before I can answer, Sam and Colette are back.

When Mia sees another woman has arrived, I can see her shrink back with dismay.

"*Mon Dieu*, what have you done to this poor girl?" Colette immediately heads straight for Mia. "Where are her clothes?" Her tirade continues with a half dozen French expletives.

She wraps her arm around Mia. "Let me get you away from this jackass," she says.

"I have things in the car," Mia says.

"She got hit by a poison dart," I mention, rubbing the back of my neck.

"And all her clothes flew off?" Colette shoots back.

There is no point in arguing with an irate Colette. I step back as they pass me for the door. Colette scoops up the shoes on the way.

Sam shakes his head. When they are gone, he says, "That one's going to cause you trouble."

"What do you mean?" Sam couldn't know who Mia is.

"You can't take your eyes off her," he says. "How did you sneak a Phase One out of training?"

"She has the shoes, but she's civilian," I say, trying to sound nonchalant.

"Not your usual type," he says, leaning against

the barn wall. He glances around. "Nor your usual venue. What happened at the silo in St. Louis?"

"Didn't go well," I say.

"Big surprise," Sam says. "Saw the alert ordering you to New Attica. That's one hell of a prison."

I pick up the axe again and turn it over in my hand. "They wouldn't listen."

"Tried to tell you, boss."

I shake my head. "Doesn't make sense. Klaus was killed. His record was deleted. Then the safe-house records were altered."

Sam shakes his head. "Ain't nobody got the clearance for that. Not even Sutherland himself."

"Exactly. And it reminds me of another bit of tampering."

"You mean Jovana and that dude you killed."

"Singer," I say grimly. His death still weighs on me. "Elroy Singer."

"He was a punk anyway," Sam says.

"Vigilante punk."

"Still a punk." Sam peers out the barn door. "We can't stay long with her car. We're too close to your rendezvous with the silo."

"I assume they aren't on to me since I

jettisoned the Crybaby."

"Am I good or am I good?" Sam's teeth flash white in the dim barn. "You got a plan?"

"I'm planning to take Mia back to the safe house," I tell him.

If she'll go, I think silently. That girl is determined to stay on my tail. That's why I pulled back in the hay when I realized she was a virgin. She'll get attached, and I don't need her as a liability with everything going on.

"Colette can do that," Sam says. "Do we need to do one of your covert exits?"

I grunt out a short laugh. Sam has gotten me out of a lot of tight spots, and some of them have involved extricating myself from an overexuberant female.

"Maybe," I say.

"She seemed a little miffed."

"She has her heart set on going with me."

"Ah," Sam says. "Looks like she's all dressed now."

Colette and Mia come back in the barn. Colette tosses me a shirt and pushes the door a little wider to get more light in.

"Colette, I'm going to need you to take Mia

back to the safe house," I say, setting down the axe so I can dress.

"What?" Mia interjects. "I thought after —" She sputters out, not wanting to say what she did in hopes of earning a place with me.

"You thought wrong," I say firmly. "Colette will see you home." I slip on the shirt and start buttoning it. "Sam, I assume my car is all right for you to ride in for a while?"

"I'll activate my secondary clone ID," Sam says. "That'll buy us some time."

"Where are you going?" Colette asks. "Should I meet up with you?"

Mia looks from one to the other like she's watching a tennis match. Her anger is about to turn to tears. I need out of here before that happens.

"We'll let you know," I say. "Sam will rig something up for communication."

"I saw you lost both my Blackphone AND my Crybaby," Sam says. "I'm not giving you anything good anymore."

I clap him on the back. "Sure you will." I head toward the door.

"You're not even going to say good-bye?" Mia's voice is tremulous.

Colette wraps her arm around Mia's shoulders. "That rat isn't worth the words," she says. "Jax De Luca, I'm ashamed of you. This poor wretched girl."

But Mia doesn't like that either. She shrugs Colette away. "I'm not wretched, and I'm not a girl."

She storms past all of us and out into the yard.

"Not sure where she's going," Sam says. "Unless she's going to hitchhike."

"Go pick her up," I tell Colette.

"I'm not fond of cleaning up your messes," she says.

"This one is unusual," I say. "She wants to be a Vigilante and doesn't understand how things work."

"I see," Colette says. "All right. I'll take her back." She steps up to me and pokes my shirt. "But you better turn over a new leaf. I'm not going to let young innocents get brokenhearted because you had bad judgment with that other woman."

I hold up my hands. "Understood."

Sam shakes his head. "Jax, my man, you have got to get your pecker under wraps."

I almost correct him on this matter, but decide it's best just to let it go.

5

MIA

I've never been more grateful for a pair of stolen shoes in my life.

The Phase One Trainee sneakers are like walking on air, even if I am leaving in a huff from a barn in the middle of God-knows-where, just minutes after my first orgasm.

My face blazes just thinking about it.

Then he rejected me.

God.

Thankfully the blazer that came with the navy

pantsuit is heavy enough for the blustery wind. In the sun, I'm relatively warm, but as I pass the shadow of the old house, I shiver.

The three of them are talking at the barn still. Jax wants to pawn me off on that French woman. She's nice, but I'm not going to do anything he says again.

Ever.

The ground crunches beneath my shoes as I head up the long drive. I'll get to the road, stick out my thumb, and start another life of danger. I'll hitchhike with truck drivers.

So there.

They'll probably try to do something to me, though.

Ugh.

This line of thought takes me straight back to the barn, and Jax hovering over me, hands working, his beautiful face inches from mine.

Damn it.

I want the rest of it. Him naked too. All the things lovers do.

My body flushes hot.

Gah. This isn't helping.

The trees rustle overhead. They tower on either

side of the long drive like soldiers. This must have been an amazing homestead at one time.

A car rumbles up behind me. It's probably Jax and his fancy friends, all jetting off to their next big adventure. Danger that I'm too sweet and innocent for, apparently.

I am the one who got us out of that stupid silo. I was the special one with the security bracelet.

I didn't panic when we went up a dark ladder or jumped off a cliff into a river. I kept up with him when we ran through the woods.

Although I guess I am also the one who almost got us caught in the car.

Now I'm back to how it felt to be with Jax, sitting in his lap, tying his arms over his head. He may have taught me how to focus and untie myself, but I have so much more to learn. Who knows, maybe I even know a knot or two to show him.

Damn it.

The car slows down as it approaches. The window rolls down. It's not Jax's car, but a silver BMW.

"Mia!" Colette calls. "Please get in!"

I ignore her, looking stubbornly ahead. I don't want her to have to take me home. I'm going to do it myself, even if some skanky truck driver tries to fondle me.

Maybe I'll let him. Take that, Jax.

Colette angles her car to my side of the road and cuts me off. I halt, surprised she could maneuver the car so effectively.

I back up, planning to circle the BMW, but she does it again, cornering the car hard so that the fender brushes my fingers. She's that close.

I head for the trees. She can't reach me in there. But she jets forward and practically circles me to cut me off from that direction. I've never seen anyone move a car like that.

So I stop.

"Is that your superpower?" I call out. "Making a car skip around like a punch-drunk squirrel?"

Her high laughter makes me smile even if I am miffed. "You are so adorable. I see why Jax is so enraptured by you."

Jax? Enraptured?

The side door pops open on its own. I want to hear more about this, so I decide to get in.

The interior of this car is not as posh and supple as Jax's Lexus, but it's sporty and fun. The leather seats are dark red. The dash is silver. "Do you have all the fancy stuff Jax has in his car?" I ask.

"Way more," Colette says as we speed down the drive and careen around a curve. "Jax's car is a retrofit. This is Vigilante from the ground up."

I reach for a seat belt, then realize there isn't an ordinary buckle.

"Oh, here," Colette says, and presses one of what must be a hundred buttons on her dash.

I hear a buzz near my ear and a beam of light crosses my shoulder, follows the curve of my chest, and goes down to my waist.

"Is it a laser seat belt?" I ask.

"Oh, no," Colette says with another merry laugh. "It's just assessing what level of safety is most optimum for your size."

After a second, another buzz makes me turn my head. This time it's a belt, not made of a fabric weave like traditional ones, but a rubbery silicone. It is pre-shaped to my body.

"Strange," I say as the metal clasp jets across my body, then finds its mate on the seat. For a moment it fits loosely, then it snaps into place.

I've never felt so firmly secured in a car. Against my back, I can feel the seat shifting to adjust just for me.

For a moment, I think it's going to force me to sit pressed into the cushion the whole time, but when I lean forward, it allows me to move, just like an ordinary belt.

"This system keeps you safe when you ride with a Phase Six Driver like me," she says. "I'm authorized to drive up to sixteen hundred kilometers per hour." She pauses. "That's about one thousand miles per hour for you Americans."

"Cars can go that fast?" I ask. "Do race car drivers go that fast?"

"The current world record for land speed is 750 miles per hour," she says. "But Vigilante drivers consider that a toddler on a trike."

I hold on to the belt with both hands. "Are we going to go that fast?"

"Not in this car, sadly. No jets. But don't worry, we are in no hurry to get you to the safe house." She presses several buttons and a screen blips on. It reads "Eight miles to rendezvous with clone identity."

"What does that mean?" I ask. I want to learn it all. Maybe I can convince this Colette person to keep me on. I wouldn't lose Jax then.

"I attached my identification to another person so I could meet Jax without the network knowing," she says. "He's not exactly on their good side at the moment."

"How is it that you can defeat their security so easily?" I ask.

"Oh, it's not easy, that's for sure," she says. "But Jax was a director, in line to take over the entire American syndicate. That got him some very high-level assistance, people like Sam, who can circumvent the very technology he invented."

"And you? Are you special too?" I ask.

"Not particularly," she says. "But I can do this." She veers off the highway and we're in the forest. Somehow she dodges trees, swerving right and left. Small branches whip against the windshield.

Then we hit a clearing and a small pond. She aims right for it.

I stifle a squeal but the car keeps going.

Right across the pond.

"Jesus," I say.

"Literally," she adds merrily, still concentrating. Ahead is an outcropping that erupts from the ground with enormous jagged rocks.

She slams the brakes and stops the car inches from it.

"How did you do that?" I turn around to look at the water, thinking it must be a mirage.

"All our cars are amphibious," she says.

I place my hands against the dash. "Can this one fly?"

"Ah, you are excited by the possibilities, no?" Colette lets out another of her infectious laughs. "A Vigilante never reveals all her tricks!"

"How long have you been a Vigilante?" I ask.

"Since I was fourteen," she says. She presses another button and after a moment, another car comes from behind the rocks. The driver waves to her.

On the dash, her screen says, "Identity reinstated."

"I'm me again!" she says. She backs away from the cliff and circles the pond this time. "I stole a military tank when I turned twelve and drove it up the Champs-Élysées — a very important street in Paris."

We head back through the trees, more leisurely this time. "My *maman* knew I had a fantastic career ahead of me as a Vigilante driver. Both my parents were in the network."

"How did you end up in America?" I ask.

"Jax recruited me. He likes the idea of crossing the networks," she says.

"Is that why Klaus was German?"

She frowns. "Yes. Klaus was very thorough, very good. He had a level of focus that isn't as easy to come by in the States. Security was his strength."

"I'm sorry that he's dead."

We bump back onto the road.

"Well, we must learn what happened to him." She gives me a wan smile. "And for that, we must get back to your home. Find the clues."

"Will Jax come?" I hate myself for asking, but I am desperate to know.

She winks at me. "For you, yes, I think he will come."

The edges of her screen blink red. "Uh-oh," she says. "What is this?" She taps the screen.

A clipped male voice says, "Encrypted transmission. Are you secure?"

"I have a civilian in my car," she says. "A Mia—" she stops. "What is your last name?" she asks.

Before I can answer, a gray-haired man's face

fills the screen. “You have Mia Morrow, who is a person of interest to the network,” he says, then his eyes move over to me.

I realize he can see us, and I self-consciously smooth my hair, realizing too late that there are bits of hay in it.

“Ms. Morrow,” he says. “I deeply regret that your safety was compromised in one of our silos.” He must feel he is imposing on the small screen, as he shifts back, revealing his shoulders and the breast of a smart navy suit. I’d put him close to sixty, but fit and handsome.

He continues. “Jax De Luca is a dangerous fugitive who unfortunately has intimate knowledge of our security systems.”

“I’m all right,” I say.

He turns to Colette. “Where did you find her?”

“Walking along a drive about twenty miles from this location,” Colette says.

A husky male voice comes from the dash. “Mood sensor activated.”

The man onscreen pauses a moment, his arms crossed over his chest. Colette smiles cheerily as she continues to drive as if nothing is happening. I don’t dare ask her what it means.

After a moment, the man says, "Good, I'm glad you are telling the truth and not covertly assisting your former director."

"Of course!" Colette says brightly. "Poor girl was wandering about. I saw the alert on Jax. What did he do this time?"

"It isn't a critical issue at the moment," the man says, his eyes flicking to me. "Where are you taking Ms. Morrow?"

"She says she lives in Tennessee. We're headed there."

"Very good," he says. "Make sure her home is secure and set up monitoring."

"I don't want to be watched!" I say. If Jax comes, they'll find him!

"I assure you, your privacy is our utmost concern," the man says. "It is only for your protection."

"Who are you?" I ask, and not especially nicely.

"I apologize. I am Jacob Sutherland, Director of the United States Security Division of Special Forces." He smiles.

It's not lost on me that he doesn't mention the Vigilantes. Everyone wants to think I'm ignorant.

"Who ARE you people?" I ask, deciding to continue the ruse.

Colette glances at me, then her attention returns to the road.

Sutherland holds out his hands in a friendly gesture. "We are a government agency that manages national security," he says smoothly.

"How did I get mixed up in this?" I ask. If he's going to be generic, then I can be nosy.

"You were captured by one of our rogue operatives," he says. "Did you see the Bourne movies?"

Ugh. Now he's insulting me. "No," I say with disdain. Our life has been nothing like a movie.

He laughs. "Jax is no longer part of a rather secret program." His face shifts into seriousness. "I hope we can count on you for discretion."

"Of course," I say absently.

"Take her home," he says to Colette. "Thank you for your service."

Colette gives a salute. The screen goes blank.

I'm about to say something when she gets a word in first. "They'll be listening in on our conversation during the drive," she says. "For your safety."

Sam rolls his eyes. "All you had to do was disconnect it, not yank it out like Mola Ram."

"Who?"

"Mola Ram. Old *Indiana Jones* character. You know, pulled out a dude's heart?" He holds his hand up in a claw grip and I shake my head.

"Never mind," he sighs. "Just don't do it again. This thing is a bitch to get back in."

"I'll remember that the next time I've got a dying woman in the backseat and enemies breathing down my neck," I say.

Sam grunts in reply, then tosses me a transmitter. "Rewire and reboot," he says and busies himself with finishing his more intricate work.

I snatch up a wire cutter and sit on an overturned wood crate to unsnarl the mess I made when I jerked everything free.

My mind turns back to Mia. She and Colette should be on their way to Tennessee by now. What will Colette tell her? She's never been a fan of my exploits, but to my knowledge she's also never badmouthed me to anyone in the past.

I shouldn't care what Mia thinks of me. I don't expect to see her again. It's best for both of us if she stays far away.

I strip a wire and attach it back to the transmitter. The Vigilantes keep tabs on everybody, and Mia in particular. That bracelet they gave her was beyond anything I ever issued to anyone when I was a silo director. It worked on doors that the skeleton key didn't budge. That kind of unfettered access was typically only available to top-level officials and special guests.

Sutherland would be the only one with that kind of power.

Mia was, by all evidence, just an innocent who got wrapped up in something over her head. An innocent with a wiped record. Which could only mean she had contact with the Vigilantes in the past. Unknowingly, most likely.

I shake my head. No, Jax. This is just wild speculation. She may have ambition and some raw talent, but she's not Vigilante material. And if her wiped record and the bracelet are any indication, that was a decision made long ago.

She's safer having nothing to do with us. With me.

"All right, I think I got it," Sam calls out from the car. He pulls out a thin black slab from his bag as he approaches and hands it to me. "Your new

Blackphone. Don't lose this one. It's completely blank. All untraceable materials."

"So I'm solidly off grid?" I slip the phone into my pocket.

"Except to me and Colette," Sam says, nodding. "Even then, you come up as unknown. Which reminds me," he adds with a glance at his watch. "We need to get moving. My clone's ticking."

"All right," I say, and slip into the driver's seat.

Sam pulls out a tablet, then tosses the bag in the backseat. He slides into the passenger seat so recently occupied by Mia. I push the thought out of my head and start the car.

"All systems check out. We are clean," Sam says as he taps on his tablet. "What's the plan?"

"We need to find someplace we can log into the network anonymously," I say. "We need to find out exactly what happened to Klaus." My hands tighten on the steering wheel. "And find Jovana."

"Yeah, about Klaus," Sam says with a singsong lilt. "I'm not sure he's actually dead."

"What?" I stare at him. Is he joking? "I saw the record. He died at the Tennessee safe house. Mia's house." *I even thought for a while she had done it*, I add silently.

"Yeah, but something's not right with that record," Sam replies. "When you sent that message, I was shocked and starting digging. I couldn't figure out how Colette and I had not seen that before."

"It was hidden," I say. "Carter, the director of that silo, had to search for editing flags to even find it."

"And that's just it," Sam says. "Why hide something like that?"

I start to reply but stop. Sam's nod tells me he's already been down this path.

"So if you want to make someone disappear," Sam continues, "a faked death is one way to do it. But the records are still there, so you have to hide those, too." His face is solemn. "That's some high-level shit, Jax. And why go to that trouble if the person is really dead?"

Of course.

7

Mia

We arrive at my aunt's house in the early evening. Colette has been witty and funny despite the fact that we had to limit our topics of conversation. We ate at a burger joint and she made fun of the French fries.

I'm glad to be out of the car for a while. My life has been nothing but long drives and difficult conversations for what seems like ages.

Colette pulls up in front of the porch. Nothing about the house looks any different, but my perspective of it certainly is. Everybody says it's a safe house for Vigilantes. They can't all be wrong.

I must be the one who's wrong.

I realize I don't have any keys and the front door has all six deadbolts in place. I can't remember if Jax locked the back door or not. Seems like he would have given me the keys if he'd had them.

"We'll have to go around back," I tell Colette.

She walks from the car and smooths her smart beige sweater, making sure the navy stripe along the bottom edge is flat. Do all these Vigilantes dress like models?

She follows me around the house. "I'm guessing Jax stole you and snuck out the back like a common criminal."

"Something like that," I murmur, remembering my tattered gown and the red ropes.

The back door is closed but unlocked.

"Let's take some care going in," Colette says. "Let me go first."

She pulls a gadget from her pants pocket. It looks like a Swiss army knife, but when she flips it, something that resembles the barrel of a gun pops out.

Colette eases the door open. I wince when it

squeaks on its hinges.

She steps inside, then pauses, listening.

Once we're in the kitchen, she shakes her sleeve so that it falls back, revealing a watch a lot like the one Jax had before we went to the silo. With one tap, it scans the room with a strange gold light. Certain things turn red. The coil beneath the refrigerator. My radio clock with its digital display. Then a strange lump below the oven.

"What's that?" I whisper.

"I think you have a mouse," she says.

I suppress a squeal. "I do not."

She moves to the door, but I continuc to stay by the oven, feeling freaked out. I tap lightly on the side of the stove. A tiny scuffle below makes me want to jump on a chair.

Instantly I'm annoyed with myself. I just escaped a high-security silo, swam in a river, and tried to seduce a dangerous man.

I will not freak out about a mouse.

Colette moves to the next room, but my mind is still admittedly on the critter in my house. I've been here for six months while I nursed my aunt as she faded away. I never saw any evidence of mice.

I turn on the light over the stove.

But I see it now.

The package of bread on the counter has a hole in it, and little dribbles of dried crumbs litter the surface.

What's different now, since I left? Is it just because the house was never empty before? It was only one night.

I spot a bit of rice on the floor near the pantry. That shouldn't be there either.

The door is slightly ajar and I open it wider. I never leave that door open and I'm quite certain I didn't before I went to bed last night, before Jax arrived.

I step inside and flip on the light. A bag of rice also has a hole, more grains spilling out. Two cereal boxes are turned on their sides.

Dang it. How am I going to get rid of it? Trap it? Maybe I can borrow someone's barn cat.

I lean my head against the door frame. I don't want to be here. I don't want to deal with a big empty house alone. My need for Jax rises up, overwhelming me. It's ridiculous. I barely know him. He was horrid to me. Tied me up. Stole me. Then foisted me off on his friend.

But the things he made me feel. So much

power. And passion. This can't be very common, what has happened between us.

Maybe it is for him. Maybe all his women feel like I do when he leaves.

I kick at the rug that has been on the floor of this pantry since I was a child. I cock my head. It's turned the wrong way.

No one would notice but me. But there's a frayed corner from where the door always catches the edge.

And that corner is opposite the door now, near the back wall.

Someone's moved this rug since yesterday.

I want to back out of there, call for Colette. Fear sluices through me as I think about some stranger going through my things.

But then I remember — Jax.

Maybe it was just him. I think he said he looked around.

I pick up the end of the rug and slide it back.

And then I see it.

A hatch.

There's something hidden in this pantry.

Colette is no longer quiet, and I hear her footsteps coming up the hall. "All clear!" she calls.

I shove the rug back in the pantry and close the door.

She pops her head in the room. "You okay?"

"Just the mouse," I say, gesturing toward the bread on the counter. "I hate mice."

"Get a kitty," Colette says. She turns on the overhead light. "Cozy little place."

"It's been my aunt's forever," I say. "Why do you people keep calling it a safe house?"

"Never mind all that. Sounds like a miscommunication from the beginning." Her smile is genuine, even though I know she's lying. "Jax wrote letters to the wrong place."

"No," I insist. "Jax said Klaus was killed here. He was very clear about it."

Colette stares up at the ceiling. "You know, I think I saw a cat wandering in the field behind your house. You want to go see? She will help with the mouse problem."

What? I stare at her, and her eyes get very big. She taps her forehead. "You want that, right? A cat for the mouse?" she says.

She heads for the back door, and I start to understand. We're being monitored here, just like in the car.

"That's a great idea," I say.

We leave the house and walk a ways through the field. Aunt Bea's land stretches for several acres, a buffer against the rest of the world.

And easy to defend, I realize, seeing the house and fields through new eyes. It's flat and easy to spot people arriving. There aren't any trees or places to hide.

Did she know and never told me?

"How does a Vigilante stop being a Vigilante?" I ask suddenly.

Colette stops and turns to me. Her short bob swings against her cheekbones. She slides her sleeve up and taps her watch. Only when it tells her what she wants to know does she answer. "You can retire, just like with anything."

"Does your family have to know you are one?"

"It's through your family that you become one," she says. "Why all the questions?"

"Why didn't I know this was a safe house?"

"Only your aunt could answer that." Colette's dark eyes search the fields and follow a car that drives along the road in the distance. "But there are parents who retire and never tell their children."

"My parents are dead."

This gets her attention. "How did they die?"

"Boating accident."

Her lips push together in a tight line.

"I know," I say. "It's like a spy cliché. But they were huge regatta racers. They liked boating in storms. They lived for that sort of danger. It was really only a matter of time."

She nods absently, eyes back on the road. "There are reasons for everything," she says. "Do you have the option of selling this house and moving?"

"I hadn't thought about it yet," I say. "Aunt Bea only died a couple weeks ago."

"You have no other family?"

I shake my head. "No. My father was an only child, and Aunt Bea was my mother's sister."

Colette reaches out to squeeze my arm. "You really are alone in this world, aren't you?"

It sounds so bleak when she says it. "I want to go with Jax," I tell her. "I have nothing else."

She sighs and starts a slow walk back. "Jax is a charismatic man," she says. "No one ever wants to leave him."

I picture all the women she is probably talking about and frown, but I step alongside her. The cold, stiff weeds crunch as we step on them.

I don't really want to go back to the silence of my house, although I am anxious to explore the pantry. But if Colette leaves, so does my only connection to Jax.

"Can I go with you?" I ask her.

"Not possible," she says. "They'd just take you from me and bring you back anyway."

"The Vigilantes, you mean?" I ask.

She nods. "You're seeing way more of it than you should."

"What will happen now?"

She pauses again and reaches out to stop me from walking farther.

I sense we are just out of range of whatever devices are inside my house that monitor my activity. I make note of the location and draw a circle in my mind around the perimeter so I can remember.

"I think you should sell this house and move on with your life," Colette says.

"But someone else will end up here."

"It will get bought by the people who need it."

"Oh." I guess the Vigilantes can do anything they want.

She starts back to the house.

"Will I be able to get hold of Jax?"

She shakes her head. "Nobody gets in touch with him unless he wants it."

"Can I get in touch with you?"

Colette stops again. "Mia, I'm sorry Jax mixed you up in this. I know it looks like an exciting life. But there's no way to let you in. I'm sorry."

We head back in silence, finally arriving on the back porch. Her voice changes to something more formal, like her words are being monitored for quality assurance.

"We have some security that will watch over you," she says. "But they are not invading your privacy. No one is recording your activity or listening in. They just pay attention to who might arrive and make sure they are not a problem."

If they're not listening, then why is she talking like this? My hair prickles on my neck.

"Would that happen?" I ask. "Would somebody come here?"

She hesitates. "No. You will be safe." She leans forward and kisses me on one cheek, then the other. "Take care, Mia."

Then she's walking to her car.

I watch the fancy BMW fire up and head down the lane. I don't go in the house right away. I plunk down on the porch step. I feel absolutely bereft. She's my only connection to Jax. And now she's gone. They're all gone.

I lean my head against the banister and let myself fall into a nice hard pity party. I'm alone. Nowhere to go. Nothing but this rambling house that somehow brought Jax to me only to have him leave again. There's no way to find him. If the Vigilantes can't track him, then I have no hope.

I stand up again. Unless there's something in the pantry that can help me.

I have to look.

8

JAX

I figure Mia is home by now. It's been six hours.

Sam guides us to a Vigilante outpost that is hidden beneath a donut shop. I'm sitting out in the parking lot with an ancient heat cloak blocking my body signature.

Meanwhile, Sam's inside ordering a cinnamon roll.

The cloak is stifling with the sun coming through the window. It has a clear pane I can see through, but I feel like a damn antique sitting here with it.

Sam has stolen and repaired too much tech since I've been out of prison, and he's not pleased with how I destroyed his last efforts.

Therefore, I'm stuck under an old cloak that smells like Old Spice.

My thoughts keep straying to Mia. I wonder what she's up to, back at home, puttering around her rambling old house.

Because I have nothing else to do, I pull out an IdentiPad and look up Georgiana Powers, who ran that safe house until the period where Klaus arrives and is reported dead. The house is decommissioned and Powers leaves.

Meanwhile, I'm in jail and don't know any of this and send letters to Klaus at this house. Mia gets them and writes back.

I can't concentrate.

My mind drifts to her last letter, the sentence she had written when I found her at the safe house. Something about ripping her gown to expose her naked hips.

I picture her in the barn, lying in the hay, her wrists tied over her head. Every wiggle makes her breasts sway deliciously, and her body is warm around my fingers.

Focus, Jax.

I won't see her again. Normally this isn't an issue. The women through the years are a blur. Vegas. LA. New York. Berlin. Paris.

But something about Mia is different. It's better I stay far away.

I keep reading. Was Georgiana Mia's aunt?

Georgiana Powers was born to two Vigilantes and entered the program in 1960 at the age of fifteen. Her stellar record during the Vietnam War got her Phase Six status by the age of twenty with a specialty in long-range weapons.

Then her parents were seriously injured in action and took charge of the safe house as a semi-retirement. They were only nominally involved with the network, since that safe house was rarely used.

Georgiana took over the house in the late '70s and stayed there until her health failed six months ago.

I set down the pad. The information matches the timeline Mia told me. But there is no mention of a sister or a niece. Maybe all that was wiped when Mia was declared a special.

The door opens and Sam gets back in the car.

"Easy as pie," he says as he starts the car. "Two Vs are stationed here during the day, mostly monitoring system backups." He grins. "Which means we have backups."

He exits the parking lot. When we get out on the road, he says, "You can take that cloak off now."

I pull the damn thing down, sweat trickling down my neck. "Why wasn't your car cloaking me?"

Sam laughs. "It was."

"What the hell?"

"Just a little joke since you're causing me all this trouble."

Asshole. "So who's there at night?" I ask. Back to business.

Sam smacks his hands on the steering wheel. "That's the beauty. They rely on electronic surveillance. Nobody thinks these old backups are worth the manpower."

I toss the cloak in the backseat. "When do we head back?"

"Just after midnight," Sam says.

I stare out the window. The pine trees whizzing

by still make me think of Mia. Probably I'll never come through this part of the country again without picturing her in that field behind a tractor, strips of her gown falling off her body to the ground.

But she's safe now.

9

MIA

The rug slides easily out of the pantry and into the kitchen. I kneel on the floor, running my fingers along the edges of the hatch door. There is no obvious way to open it. The floor is smooth other than the rectangular crack.

There has to be a way. I'm willing to bet a lot of money that the mouse got into the house when Jax opened this door, and then the little guy got stuck in my kitchen, unable to get back. I suppress a shudder. I will not be afraid of a mouse.

I crawl along the floor. The hatch is fairly big, a couple feet wide and probably four feet long. I wonder if it's like those old stereo cabinets that didn't have a handle. You had to press the right spot to trigger a mechanism to make them pop open.

Hopefully there's not some spy gadget required to unlock it.

I spend a solid half hour pressing on sections of the hatch, and still nothing. Now I'm starting to suspect that there's a lever hidden somewhere, like a secret bookcase that opens when you pull on the right book.

But this pantry has been thoroughly cleaned out. I spent hours a day doing it while Aunt Bea was sick. I had little else to do. I don't think there's a single jar or box or shelf that wasn't moved or touched during that time.

I plop down on the floor, frustrated. I don't want to rip out the wood planks, but if that's what it takes, I will do it. I have an axe in the outside shed.

The thought of an axe makes me picture Jax in the barn, shirtless, wielding one when we were interrupted in the hay.

It's fully dark now, so maybe all this can wait until morning. I feel a little spooked about walking outside. Even though Colette said the house was being watched, I can't help but wonder who the real enemy is.

If only Jax would come. I wonder if he is like that vampire in *Twilight*, the one who liked Bella. She put herself in danger on purpose, just to make him show up to save her.

But then, Edward actually loved Bella.

Jax doesn't care one whit about me. He pawned me off on Colette the first chance he got.

Even after what happened in the hay.

And what *didn't* happen.

I wander the house, turning on every single light. The solitude is suffocating. When I get to the bedroom, my throat tightens at the sight of the letters still scattered on the bed and floor. The sheets are all askew. I sit down and pick up one of the pages. My heart squeezes as I read a line.

Along the smooth plane of your naked back, I tie a lover's knot, one side black, the other red.

I set it back down. No more letters. No more excitement. No more Jax.

I peel off the pantsuit from Armond. I have

another long white nightgown like the one Jax destroyed, but I leave it in the drawer. I put on a pair of flannel pajamas instead. I don't even know what to do now, so I pick up all the letters and tuck them back inside the box on my side table.

The wind rushes against the window, making me shiver. I have always liked being alone, but I don't now.

I flop backwards on the bed and stare at the ceiling. At least I have the memories. I sort through each moment from that first night. Waking up. Seeing Jax at the end of the bed, my ankle on his shoulder. His knife slicing through my gown, right until we heard the alarm —

I sit up straight. The lampshade. It had some sort of device in it.

I hurry over to it. I peer inside, but all I can see are ordinary things. The off-white shade. Wires that hold it in place. The bulb and the screw top where it attaches to the pole. A heavy base and the wire to the wall.

That's right. Jax took the alarm with him. It was small and oval.

I close my eyes and try to picture it. I was terrified then, but it still sticks in my mind.

There has to be another one somewhere.

I head into my aunt's old bedroom, where two lamps flank her oversized bed. Sorrow wells up that she is no longer there. Even her frail body tucked under the covers was a type of company. I still had someone.

I wonder what she would think if she could see me now.

I check the lamps. The first one has nothing in it.

But in the second? Yes. There it is. Another small oval device attached to the wire, pressed against the shade so you wouldn't notice it.

I pull it out and hold it in my hand. Will it know I've found it? Does it have a heat sensor or motion detector?

No alarm goes off. Nothing happens. I examine it closely. Jax said it was seriously old tech. It's just a piece of plastic, maybe half an inch thick, shaped like an oval. There's a little vent on the bottom. I guess that lets the sound come out for the alarm.

It must have some sort of sensor inside.

I should smash it, look at its insides. But I don't know what that would tell me. I couldn't do anything smart like reverse engineer the receptor so that I could see where the signal comes from, how it knows the house is compromised.

Besides, this wouldn't bring me Jax. It would only alert more people like the silo guards or that Sutherland man.

Still, this bit of plastic, cold and hard, is my only connection to the Vigilantes. The only proof that they are real. I hold it tight and take it back to my bedroom.

I go to sleep with all the lights on, and the alarm beside me on the pillow.

10

JAX

The donut shop is silent and still when Sam pulls up. "I'll buzz you when I have the heat detectors down," he says. "Then you can stroll in."

I watch him as he crosses the lot and deactivates the door locks. He pauses by a plastic bin and peers inside, extracting a bear claw from beneath a sign that says "Day-old pastries."

That Sam.

He disappears through swinging doors behind the counter.

This part of town is quiet and dark. It's a poor section, judging by the sagging facades of the buildings, and the asphalt outside the car is cracked and broken. This donut shop isn't a chain, but some mom-and-pop shop. Probably retired Vigilantes who wanted a small business. Since they're covering for an outpost, they don't even have to turn a profit. Just make their pastries and work whatever hours suit them.

Easy life.

Not for me. But easy.

The screen on the dash lights up. Sam's face appears. "Come on in, boss. Don't forget to activate the clone ID."

I click on the key chain that bears the electronic signature of a young man whose Vigilante status is pending. The records will show him coming into service about 24 hours earlier than he is actually activated, but this window allows me to come into an outpost without incident.

I enter the door and am hit with the powerful scent of sugar. Working with Sam is always a trial of fighting junk food. Once he officially hit Phase Ten as a tech guy, he was eligible to skip ongoing military training.

And he did. Best day of his life, he claims.

I prefer to stay in solid fighting shape, regardless of my class.

Just beyond the swinging doors is a pantry. Inside it is an elevator.

This must be the way.

Like most Vigilante elevators, there are no buttons. If you get in at the top, you get out at the bottom. It's a steel trap with no emergency exits. Most are equipped with gas jets as well, whatever poison the Vigilantes want to give you, nerve or sleeping or laughing or death.

The car stops and the doors slide open. Sam is hunched over a keyboard connected to six older-model screens.

No slick glass displays here. Not surprising, since it's a storage for backups. The room is bare, just concrete walls lined with wires that lead to this main console. Off to one side are metal cabinets that house more backup units. Still, there will be hidden security.

"Klaus is gone from the system like you said," Sam says, munching on the pastry as he scrolls through code. "He exited six months ago with his death at the safe house."

"What about before?" I drop onto a stool next to Sam.

"I pulled the backups. It's all the stuff we know. You nabbed him from the German syndicate. Lots of our exploits in Vegas. Your move to the West Coast syndicate and hiring him on."

"What about the night I killed Singer? He was there."

"Nothing in the system or on backup."

"Jovana?"

Sam taps at the keys. "Still has the special status she had when you were with her. No records."

Damn. "Look up anything else that might have been deleted the day Klaus was reported dead."

Sam wipes the back of his hand across his mouth. "Killer pastries here," he says as he types. "Okay, so there is some deleted security footage in the head syndicate. A meeting. Klaus was in the room. Sutherland. And a special."

"Jovana," I say.

"I'd bet on it," Sam says. "This is where they planned Klaus's disappearance. The timeline is right."

"Sutherland is in on it."

"This is bad, dude." Sam glances around at the

corners of the room. "Glad this is an old outpost. We'd be dead already if we were monitored."

"Can you trace a special even if she doesn't have a name?"

"Sure, they still have IDs." Sam's voice is strained. "This is all we should do, Jax. Now that we know how high it goes, we have to kill this query."

I nod. "Let's just check that one thing."

He taps, but his expression is grim. "Here we go. That special pops up in an altercation at an MMA fight in Vegas three months ago. Doesn't say what. But I have the date and location. Apparently there was a bit of a tiff over compromised security. Footage went viral of a couple fighting."

I lean in and note the information. "I have friends in Vegas still."

"I remember those days," Sam says. He powers the computers down. "We were always getting mixed up with the illegal MMA fights there."

"Fun times," I say.

We head back to the elevator. Sam watches the corners anxiously, and I know he's thinking about the gas.

When we're back out in the parking lot, he says, "You know I can't do a damn thing now that we know this goes to the top."

"I know it," I say. "I need to be the only dead man walking."

He claps me on the back. "Good luck, man."

I stride back to the Vigilante car. Sam looks forlorn, like he's never going to see me again.

He should know better. Nothing's gotten to me yet.

11

MIA

The next morning I head out to Aunt Bea's old shed for the axe. I sling it over my shoulder like a badass as I head back into the kitchen.

I'm going to get in that hatch, even if I have to destroy the floor.

More breadcrumbs are scattered across the counter. I should have thrown the food out. But at least if I keep the mouse fed, it will stay in this room and not explore the house.

I shudder and almost drop the axe.

Don't think about the mouse, Mia.

Still, I leave the back door open wide as an invitation for the rodent to leave. It has to be lonely, like me, all locked up with nobody to talk to.

The hatch is exactly as I left it, shut tight. I spread my feet wide, trying to get a nice steady base to strike from. I don't have a lot of space.

I raise the axe over my head and the sharp corner scrapes the ceiling, sending down a shower of plaster. I blink from the dust, resting the axe on my shoulder. Aunt Bea would kill me if she saw what I was doing to her house.

Although I guess it's mine now.

I lift the axe again, being more careful this time. Then I slam it down in the middle of the floor.

It cuts cleanly into the wood, but a ringing noise of metal on metal blasts my ears. The reverberation from the strike travels all the way up my arms.

I jerk on the axe and dislodge it from the floor. I kneel closer. A shine of steel glints between the splintered planks. The dang thing is lined with metal.

I bring the axe down again, this time shattering a plank. More of the steel door is revealed.

I keep hacking at it until most of the hatch is uncovered, hoping there will be a lock or a handle.

But even once I have a major hole, bits of wood all over the floor, I spot nothing but the crack along the rectangular edge of the metal trapdoor.

I sit on the floor among the wreckage, even more disheartened than before. My hands are screaming, red and bruised. At least two blisters are forming. I should have worn gloves.

And I have gotten nowhere. I'm no closer to opening this secret door than I was before I destroyed the floor.

I stumble to my feet and lean the axe against the shelves in the pantry. I'll clean up the mess later.

I can call someone, hire somebody who can cut metal. But I don't know what's down there. And for all I know, the people watching me would keep him from coming inside to do the job.

I have to face facts. I'm not going to be a Vigilante. I'm not going to go on more dangerous excursions or escape high-security silos.

And I will never see Jax again.

I sit at the kitchen table, picturing Aunt Bea on the other side, wearing a faded housecoat and pouring a cup of tea. My throat wells up. She was my last and only family. I'm really and truly on my own.

It's time to move on with my life. Figure out what I want to do next.

It won't be here.

12

JAX

I take it easy on the drive to Vegas, attracting no attention and trying to stay off the Vigilante radar. I obey all speed limits, pay with cash, and think over my plan of action.

And try to banish Mia from my thoughts.

Still, she creeps in at odd moments. A woman on a billboard reminds me of how Mia tilts her head when she's confused. A laugh on the radio sounds like hers.

I have to reconcile myself that I'll never see

her again. Hell, if Sutherland thinks I'm checking up on him, Sam could be right. I might not survive this thing. It's one thing to be a rogue Vigilante. It's another to be hunted by the head of the American syndicate.

It explains why he wouldn't talk to me at the silo, though, and why he ordered me to New Attica. He wants me out of the way. He always has. Clearly my position to take over his job was a threat.

But to what?

The drive, done like a normal civilian, takes almost two days. The night in the hotel is brutal, a crappy room with precious few amenities. I think of heading to a local watering hole and looking for company. I get as far as the parking lot and go to a diner instead. I have to forget about Mia first.

And I plan.

When I get to Vegas, I have to think about how to contact Antonio, an old friend who goes back as far as my Phase Six days. When I left there for the West Coast, he rose through the ranks as fast as I did. By the time I got sent to Ridley Prison a year ago, he was in line to run that syndicate.

I had to dump the clone ID when I left Tennessee, so I can't go anywhere near his silo. But because of all the years I worked the Vegas channels, I'm familiar with all the outposts and safe houses in the area.

One in particular was a favorite spot of mine when I got in a jam with the syndicate. Well outside Vegas near Lake Mead was a little old lady named Martha Clementine who ran a safe house mostly used by Phase Twos on their first missions who were feeling shaken up. Everyone called her Grandma Marty.

Marty was shrewd when it came to hiding Vigilantes from the network and giving them downtime. She got in hot water once for trading IDs, which back then were housed in our shoes for everybody, not just Phase Ones.

She would sometimes let a Vigilante take a job for one who might be struggling or was in danger of being removed from the program.

I have the technology in the car Sam outfitted for me to check and make sure her safe house is still operational and secure, but I decide against it. I'm well cloaked and even a mundane transmission like that could alert the Vigilantes to my whereabouts. I feel sure Grandma Marty will take me in if I show up unannounced. Then it's just dealing with the discretion of anyone else at the safe house.

It's late afternoon when I arrive at Lake Mead. I park near the cliffs and view the house with binoculars. The same yellow curtains hang in the front windows. She's kept up her prized white oleander bush in the yard, surrounded by the unrelenting dirt.

My best shot is to walk up without any tech. Most safe houses aren't equipped with scanners that pick up heat signatures as identifiers.

I'll pretend to be a stranded motorist in the audio. Her house is one of only three in this twenty-mile stretch of desert. It's reasonable enough.

When I walk up the road to her house, though, three Vigilante vehicles are parked under a desert camo tarp strung between the house and her shed. This makes me pause. That's a lot of witnesses. Liability.

But the woman herself comes out to empty a bucket of recovered dishwater on her oleander. She's wearing lemon-colored sweatpants and an oversized military jacket. Her hair is in rollers covered by a floral scarf.

I stride across the highway to catch her before she goes back inside.

She peers across the barren yard. "Is that you?" she asks.

"Just a stranded motorist, ma'am. Hoping you'll point me to the nearest gas station for my punctured tire." I take the bucket from her and spread the water evenly around the bush.

Marty nods knowingly. "Did you need a small service station or a full-sized outfit?"

"I'd like to talk to someone in charge."

"How bad is your flat? Might be rough weather coming." She points up, not at the sky, but at the corner of her roof.

I see the camera. It's where it always was. But she's telling me they're already listening.

"How rough?" I ask.

"People die of exposure in places like this," she says.

"I really need to talk to someone in charge since they made a rather large mistake when they sold me the tire." I set her bucket back on the ground.

"I understand what you need. Let's see what I can find. We don't have much time, though, before the storm hits." She turns and leads me to her back porch. "I assume you left your receipt in the car?"

"I did," I say. I know she's asking if I have tech on me. The woman is clever, and frankly, I'm relieved she's helping if things are as bad as she's suggesting. I don't know if she's reacting to the instructions to have me sent to New Attica, or if it's gotten worse. Grandma Marty was never one to exaggerate a threat.

"Come sit at my table," she says. "I'll find my phone book."

I hide a smirk. I always loved Marty's ruses. We go into the back of the house, and I slide into one of the orange vinyl chairs. A boy in his late teens trundles into the kitchen. Marty waves him away. "Come back in five, Ray," she says. "I've got a stranded driver in here."

The boy snatches an apple from a bowl and heads back out. I frown. Back in my training days, memorizing bulletins was an essential part of your daily duties. If this Ray kid has even looked at them, he'll know who I am.

"He's a good kid," Marty says over her shoulder as she opens a cabinet. "He never causes trouble."

I assume that means he won't report me. Probably she's protecting him from something too.

I glance around the kitchen. It's just like it always was, bright and sunny and almost completely decked out in 1970s orange. I don't know how she keeps all her aging avocado-colored appliances running. Probably any Phase Two techs who come through help her with them.

She plunks a giant 1987 set of Las Vegas yellow pages on the center of the table. Immediately, all the electronics in the kitchen go out.

"Well, look at that. Another rolling brownout." She sits down. "I have to say this fast."

I nod. Her face is drawn in concern, wrinkles collecting around her tired eyes. "I don't like this, and I'm not alone, but here it is. Someone tampered with a backup unit down south and you're being fingered for it after your Houdini in the Missouri silo."

I control my concern for Sam's safety. "They don't know who got in?"

"If they do, they're not saying. But I don't think they do. They're blaming you, regardless."

"Sutherland already ordered my apprehension for New Attica," I say.

"It's worse." She sighs. "Now it's a kill order."

The entire Vigilante network, ordered to kill me on sight.

"Thank you for not doing it," I say.

She reaches over and tweaks my ear. "You were one of my boys. I don't hold no account for them killing the likes of you, no matter what it's over."

I take her hand. "Thank you."

She squeezes my fingers. "I can't get you to Antonio, if that's what you were after. If I were you, I'd ditch everything tying you to the network, even if it's stolen or redirected. Cloaking won't help. They're double authenticating everything with a circuit, trying to ferret you out."

I nod. "Got it."

"I wish I could do more to help you," she says.

"You've done plenty." I let go of her hand.

The lights flicker and come back on.

Marty draws the book closer to her. "There's the lights. Will that number work for you? Is your cell phone charged?"

I nod. "Thank you. I'll call them straightaway."

"Take care of yourself," she says. "It's a big bad desert out there."

I walk out the back door, skirting the fringe of

the range of the cameras. They'll have me identified within ten minutes, if I have to guess. Damn. Someone will see that power drop, pull up the footage, and do a visual.

Still, Marty did me a favor. I know what I have to do now.

As soon as I'm out of camera range, I break into a run in the opposite direction of my car.

* * *

It's sixteen miles before I come across a ramshackle gas station on the highway. I've got nothing on me but my clothes and Sam's Blackphone, which I feel reasonably certain can't be traced by the Vigilantes since none of the parts or circuits came from their inventory. That's what makes it a Blackphone.

Still, I power it up only long enough to nab the number of the only person I can think of to get me information on that MMA fight in Vegas, someone outside the Vigilante network but who could access that sort of data.

The Cure McClure.

The Cure is a retired boxer in California. About

six years ago, he called on me to help locate an abducted girl, a friend of his son, Colt. Colt was big in the MMA circuit at that time, at the height of his career. Some punk hired a thug to shoot him in an alley, then tried to settle another score with another fighter who went by Power Play.

I remember the girl, black haired and fiery. Maddie was her name. She'd been through some stuff that night. But The Cure called on me for a couple other things after that, and now it is my turn to call on him.

Rather than use the Blackphone and have the use of a high-tech device be spotted so close to the compromised safe house, I head into the door of the gas station to see what I can use inside.

An old man sits behind the counter, reading a newspaper from 2009.

"Hello, sir," I say to him.

He catches me staring at the front page and shakes the newspaper so it rustles. It's a nostalgic sound.

"I share your fondness for paper," I say.

"Still can't handle those newfangled reading devices," he says. He thumbs at a pile of papers in his corner. "I figure I've got enough old news to keep me occupied till I keel over."

"Indeed you do." Quite the fire hazard as well, I want to say, but simply grab three bottles of water from a cooler.

He smacks the back of his hand against a headline. "Really funny to read a decade later about how we're all going to die of swine flu," he says. "I love this stuff."

I wait for his laughter to subside, trying not to sweat the time passing. I drop several dollars on the counter for the water.

"Where's your car?" he asks.

I down one entire bottle of water before answering. "A few miles back. I need to make a phone call, if I may," I say. "Cell phone's dead."

"All righty." He passes over his own cell. "I'd have kept my pay-phone box, but those dern workers came one night and hauled it off! Then they told me I couldn't have no landline neither. Weren't worth fixing the cables anymore." He picks up his newspaper. "Damn progress."

His phone is at least ten years old, an ancient Motorola flip. I pop it open and dial The Cure.

The voice is unhappy and harsh. "Who gave you this number?" The Cure barks.

"You did. Just before I scooped up a fighter's girlfriend who'd been abducted in Vegas." I hold my breath that he won't say my name aloud. If Sutherland has gone all-points with a kill order, they could be monitoring anyone I've ever contacted.

"James, my golden boy!" The Cure says. "I haven't seen you since you left the ring."

I release my breath. He gets it. "I'm outside Vegas and I need a ride."

"Give me the coordinates, and I'm on it."

Damn. I don't have any tech to give me my latitude and longitude. I could take a guess. I glance around the gas station. This Luddite is bound to have maps around.

Sure enough, there's a rack of faded road maps by the door. I pull one out and dust falls from the creases. It barely holds together as I unfold it.

"Searching," I tell The Cure. I find the highway I'm on and approximate the run from Grandma Marty's. "Latitude 36.206653, longitude -114.053843."

"I'll send a helicopter," The Cure says.

"I like subtlety," I tell him.

He pauses. "I'll scramble a fleet so it's not obvious."

"I appreciate it."

"Anything for a fighter boy." He hangs up.

I set the man's phone back on the counter and glance out the doors. This place won't be too hard to defend if I have to, but I hate having a civilian involved.

"Not much around these parts, is there?" I ask.

He looks up from his paper. "Only gas for fifty miles. You stranded?"

"My friend is picking me up." I spot the door to the restroom. "I'm going to make a little use of that."

"Help yourself."

In the tiny room I strip down and wash off the sweat and dust from the travels. There's probably no point in even stopping by any of my homes in New York, LA, or Detroit. A sniper would spot me before I got to the front door. There is no costume that hides a heat signature, and even Sam has never come up with a way to fake that.

When I come back out, I finish off the second bottle of water while I look out the window. It will take The Cure close to two hours to get here from LA. I need to find a defendable place and figure out what I can use as weapons, since I don't have a thing on me.

The man resumes reading his paper. I spot cigarette lighters and motor oil. If he has some twine — yes, there's a coil of it — I can oil it to be lit. Run it into the gas line.

That's all a last resort. I'm not keen on blowing up this poor man's livelihood.

I'm about to pick up the supplies when the unquestionable thrum of helicopter propellers drowns out all sound.

"That your ride?" the man asks, jumping up to look.

I peer out the window. When the dust settles, I see Colt McClure, The Cure's son, waving from the open door.

"It is. Thank you," I tell the gaping man and run toward the helicopter.

"I was in Vegas with Pop's chopper," Colt yells.

"Perfect," I say and climb into the cabin.

The pilot gives a half salute and fires the helicopter back up.

Colt leans forward in his seat. He's got on a UFC ball cap and a blue sweatshirt for some gym. I have to hope if this helicopter is suspected, the

Vigilantes won't do anything drastic with two civilians on board.

"We sent six choppers in random directions," Colt says. "Good to see you again."

"How is that lovely girl of yours?" I ask. "I didn't get to meet her in Vegas but I've seen her in the ring with you after matches." MMA fighting was popular in the viewing room at Ridley Prison.

"She's good. We're good," Colt says. "So what sort of tangle have you gotten yourself into?"

"You can't even imagine," I say, scanning the sky. A helicopter in such close proximity to that safe house and its power outage is going to be noticed. Too bad civilian copters can't be cloaked. I have to hope The Cure's idea of scrambling six of them will be effective.

I don't see any imminent danger. The skies are clear.

"Where are we headed?" Colt asks.

"I'm hoping you can tell me that," I say. "I'm trying to find a woman who was at an MMA fight in Vegas on July 28."

"Just as a spectator or does she know a fighter?"

"I'm not sure. But there was an altercation that

got caught on a lot of cell phones."

"Not sure I recall that," Colt says. "But let's see what we can track down." He opens a compartment next to his seat and lifts up a computer. "Okay, that night the lead fight was Hendrickson vs. Jones. Opener was Peters vs. Lukov."

"Lukov?" Jovana's last name is Lukova, the female version of the surname.

"Yup. He actually won that one. He was a non-UFC contender and got in on that fight."

"What's he done since then?"

"Prepared for a big match that's coming up," Colt pauses. "In two days. In Nashville."

"Can you pull up that footage from the July fight?"

"Oh, yeah, tons of hits on that if you search. It went a little viral." Colt brings up a video. The video opens with a title slide that reads "CUTE RUSSIAN GIRL SLAMS DUDE AT MMA FIGHT."

The footage starts on a fight. Some lean, muscular boy is being declared a winner. The Jumbotron above him shows his face and he points into the crowd. Whoever's filming follows his finger and there she is, Jovana, jumping up and down. Her face shows up on the giant screen.

An arm comes around her neck. I see a flash of blond hair. The image blurs, then comes back into focus as a man tries to drag Jovana from the stands.

Hell. It's Klaus. He looks rather healthy for someone who died three months prior.

The Jumbotron goes back to the fighter, but the man with his shaky phone footage stays on Jovana and Klaus. She tries to stay by her seat, but Klaus yanks on her arm. She executes a perfect judo throw, flipping him over so that he lands on his back on the stairs.

The crowd reacts, and a man's voice, probably the one making the video, says, "That had to hurt."

I bet. I was on the receiving end of one of those that last time I saw Jovana, the night I killed Singer. Despite all those months together, I didn't know she was combat trained until then.

The video ends.

"Did the woman go to his other fights?" I ask.

"No way to tell," Colt says. He does some quick searches, but nothing else comes up. "You want to go to his fight in Nashville? I can get you tickets."

I settle back in the seat. "I'll get in," I say. Forging a ticket is something I can do without any need for tech and I don't want Colt tied to me if anything goes south. "This chopper can't get as far as Nashville."

"I've made it to Albuquerque before," Colt says. "I can arrange for a car for you there, or another chopper."

"A car will do," I say. I've got two days to get to this fight, and a car is much lower profile. "Especially if you have something not in your name."

"One of those deals," he says. "I'll tell Pop." He taps out a message on his phone. "You must be in a real jam."

"Dangerous one at that. Should we drop you off?" I'm feeling concerned about defending a chopper if we're attacked in the air by Vigilantes.

"I'm all in," Colt says.

I watch out the window. Skies are still clear. Hopefully we'll make it without incident.

13

MIA

I spend a few days cleaning the house, packing up my aunt's clothes to donate, and sending off her death certificate to various banks and insurance companies to close out her estate. Soon I'll have to prepare her house for sale.

I've spotted the mouse two more times. I went into town and bought an extra loaf of bread for him. Might as well make a friend. Sometimes I laugh and call myself Cinderella.

I might be going crazy.

Josh, one of the grocery sackers, asks me out on a date. I think my neighbor Shirley put him up to it. She came over later the same day wondering if anything special had happened in town.

I want to say, sure, I got abducted by a rogue spy, stripped in a field, and had my first orgasm in a pile of hay.

This Josh guy is okay. I probably should have said yes.

Shirley's face fell when I said no, nothing happened.

I lie on my bed midafternoon one day, staring at the blue pantsuit hanging on the door of my closet. It's pretty much the only thing that ties me to Jax now. I went to the library and boldly checked out *Fifty Shades of Grey* in front of everyone. But I only got halfway through the first scene where Christian binds Ana and I had to stop. The longing got too much to bear.

I idly pick up a length of rope I keep by my bed. I've been practicing knots, over and over, tying everything I know and seeing if I can untie it again while bound. It's become something of an obsession, creating slipknots on the banister, yanking them tight, then freeing myself one-handed.

If I ever see Jax again, I think I can tie him in a way that he can't escape.

But I won't ever know. It won't happen.

I roll over and peer under the bed where I pushed Katya's stolen shoes. I've been meaning to clean them, but I'm stupidly attached even to the mud on them.

They look like such ordinary shoes, but I know better. There's no way a Phase One Trainee would have plain old sneakers.

I actually fired up Aunt Bea's ancient television and put in one of the James Bond movies she was so fond of. *Goldfinger*. In it, Bond puts a tracking device in his shoe. That movie is sixty years old, and still, they were tracking spies in shoes!

I pick up one of the dirty white sneakers. I hope Katya didn't get in trouble for losing them to me. Thinking about that makes me smile. She didn't see that coming. I wish I could have told Jax what I did.

The outside of the shoe seems normal. Leather exterior, rubber sole. A stretchy band where shoelaces normally go makes it easy to remove, but keeps it securely in place when you're wearing it.

I stick my hand inside. The interior is strange, cushioned by something unfamiliar. It almost flows against my hand, adjusting to the contours it encounters.

Like the seat in Colette's car, I realize.

The very front tip of the shoe is hard. I pull my hand out and bang the shoe on the floor. Yes, steel or something is hidden inside. Makes sense, if you're kicking in doors or fighting.

There's a lot of space between the bottom of the inside of the shoe and the base of the shoe itself.

Suddenly I realize something. There could be things hidden in there. Chips. Weapons. Trackers. I try to pull the inside layer of the shoe out, but it is well attached.

I'm torn between destroying the shoe to see what's inside, and keeping them intact. I pick up the other one to carry them to the kitchen, where I have some extra-strong shears, plus all the knives.

The pantry door is still open, the metal hatch shining on the floor. I did sweep up all the wood shards, but didn't bother replacing the rug. There's no one here to see what I've uncovered.

I wonder, if I destroy these shoes, will that bring the Vigilantes? It stands to reason that if they think one of their own has been harmed, they will come to investigate.

Do I want that? Dell or Katya or that Sutherland guy? They might send Colette again.

I set the shoes on the counter. The light is better in here, and I can see the edge of the inner lining now. I take a butter knife and pry at it, seeing if it will pull free.

After several minutes of trying, I give up and switch out for a steak knife.

I stick the blade in the seam between the edge of the shoe and the sole. At first it sinks in easily, then it hits something solid. I knew it. There's metal in there.

I slice along the heel until I can peel it up.

Holy smokes.

Beneath is a series of circuits. If I had to guess what a trainee would have, there would be some sort of tracking device, maybe a motion counter to make sure they ran their miles or whatever physical work they have to do. And surely — hopefully — something that allows them to bypass security in their own facilities. The high-tech silos use those scanners, but probably other buildings in the network have normal doors.

Like safe houses do.

I carry the shoe to the pantry and wave it around. Nothing happens. I set it on the hatch. Still nothing.

I back up and sit on a kitchen chair. Dang it. I turn the shoe over in my hand.

Wait.

It probably knows whether or not it's being worn.

I pat the sole back into place and slip the shoe on. When I stand up, the bottom forms to my foot. I walk to the other and put it on as well.

Do the shoes know I'm not Katya? I think about her. She was a little taller than me, and definitely more muscular. So she probably weighed a bit more. I look around. The radio. And the toaster. I pick them both up. That's about right. Now the shoes should register that I'm her, unless there's something trickier like a chip in her body.

It's worth a shot.

I walk toward the pantry.

My heart is pounding. I don't know if this will work. Or what I will find if it does. For all I know, Vigilantes will descend from the sky on lines from helicopters.

I step up to the pantry door.

Nothing.

I take another step closer to the hatch, until my toes are up against the crack.

And I hear a faint "click."

Oh my God.

The far side has lifted up almost an inch.

I did it!

I set the toaster and radio on a shelf and walk around the hatch to kneel before the opening. My fingers fit beneath the lip.

I lift the metal panel, grunting under its weight. When it gets about two feet up, I notice a steel bar on the side, like the ones used in old cars to prop up the hood.

It takes a lot of effort to hold the hatch door up with one arm, but I manage to pull the bar up and fit it in a carved-out hollow. I let go of the door with relief.

It's pitch black below. I need a flashlight.

I dodge the open door to run into the kitchen for one. If my heart was hammering before, it's firing like a machine gun now. The Vigilantes were right! Aunt Bea's house IS part of their network.

I stop for a second outside the pantry door.

Does that mean Aunt Bea was a Vigilante?

I don't have time to think about this. Maybe the answer is under that hatch.

I go back around to the back side. The way it opens, it creates a little space that is easy to defend.

Interesting.

I shine the light inside. There are only a few shallow steps. I kneel as far as I can in the cramped space, my feet against the back wall of the pantry, so I can peer into the hole before actually going down.

Four metal steps lead into a small crawl space. As far as I can tell, it doesn't go anywhere else. A few shelves are lined with black boxes.

I take a deep breath and shift around so my feet are on the stairs. I bump down, one step at a time, until I'm sitting on the bottom one.

I look up. If the hatch came down, would I be able to lift it back? Would I be trapped?

This idea terrifies me, so rather than looking around, I grab the closest box and bring it up the stairs. In two seconds, I'm out of the pantry and back at the kitchen table, my lungs sucking in and out like I've just come up for air.

Be brave, I scold myself. But I decide I'm not

going back down there without at least a cell so I can call someone if I'm trapped. I dash to the living room for my phone.

I tuck it in my pocket and head back to the kitchen.

The box looks insidious on my table, black and out of place with the sunny yellow curtains and cheery bird wallpaper.

I approach it warily. I unlocked the hatch without anyone arriving to stop me. No alarms have gone off. Still, I'm quite sure in some silo somewhere, it's been noted that I opened it. Though who knows? Maybe Jax disabled things when he was here. He surely didn't want to be seen.

The box is about a foot wide and two feet long. It has normal metal latches, like a briefcase. I flip them open.

Inside I find several Band-Aid trackers like the one Jax put on my neck at the hotel. Five syringes, each marked with a different-colored band. And a few other strange objects I can't identify, all small flesh-colored boxes, some on Velcro straps, others with adhesive backs. I pick one up. I can't see anything from the outside.

I figure this must be a "captive" box, full of

things to drug or track someone. I push it to the center of the table. Now for another one.

With the phone in my pocket, I feel more comfortable down in the hole. There are six other black boxes of varying sizes. I try to lift the biggest one, which is several feet long, but it's too heavy. So I open it instead.

And back up immediately.

Guns. Huge black guns with triggers and strange ammunition in black cylinders. They are laid out in green foam that is carved to fit them.

I close the box with a slam. Weapons. There are weapons under my house.

Unease trickles through me. I don't like knowing they are there.

I pick up the smallest box. Feeling creeped out by the guns, I take this one upstairs. Aunt Bea's bright kitchen helps calm me. I need a little normal, as I realize all these things were below my feet the whole time. I'm itching to talk to a Vigilante again and find out what they know. Was my Aunt Bea really this person they called Georgiana Powers?

Maybe Klaus really was here. Maybe he really was killed here.

Maybe Aunt Bea wasn't having strokes at all.

Maybe they killed her.

Now I can't concentrate on the box at all. My mind is racing.

How would I find this out? How could I know?

My breath starts coming in fits and hitches. I have to calm down or I'm going to hyperventilate.

If they came for Aunt Bea, wouldn't they come back for me? Who are these people? Why are they killing everyone?

I sink into a chair, every part of me trembling. I want Jax. I want him right now. But I don't know how to get him.

I sit there, jumping at every little sound, until the terror starts to settle into a manageable sort of low-level anxiety.

I pull the second box close to me. When I flip these latches, I have to smile at the contents. A pen. A notebook. Two men's clip-on bow ties, one black, one red. A bulky necklace that is a cluster of big red beads. And an oversized onyx ring.

I slip the ring on my finger. It's big. Really big. The black oval is set in a gold base. I try it on my thumb and it still slips off. Something about it makes me think of Jax, though, so I leave it on.

The light outside my back door clicks on,

timed for sunset. I wonder if the Vigilantes really are monitoring the room, and if they're watching me go through their things. That Sutherland guy didn't seem to want me to know anything. Colette played along when she knew they were listening.

It's all such a puzzle.

I'm tired. I close the box. Maybe I should sleep a little and go through the rest of the pantry tomorrow.

I pause by the door. Should I close the hatch? Something tells me I should. I can almost see the pulsing light on a panel somewhere, alerting someone that the door is open. I walk around to the back side and hang on to the heavy lid as I let the bar fall. Then I lower the hatch into place.

The two black boxes seem obvious on my counter. If Shirley comes over, which inevitably she will, she'll ask about them. I open a low cabinet and hide them inside.

I shove the rug by the back door as though I'm about to take it out for a cleaning. Now everything seems normal.

I clasp my hand around the black ring as I head back to my room. Too little sleep. Too little food. Coming down from that crazy freak-out I had when

I saw the guns. I need to rest.

Tomorrow I can figure out what I'm doing next. How to find Jax. I know he doesn't want me. But I want him. I should never have walked out of the barn. I should have made Colette take me back.

I gave up too easily.

I kick off the shoes, mad at myself. I'm going to fix this. I'm going to find my way back to him.

I don't bother shutting off any lights anymore. I can sleep fine in brightness and it's too uncomfortable to be alone in the dark. Especially now that I know about the guns. Maybe tomorrow I'll try to figure out how to use one.

Or not. God. It's so frightening.

Jax invades my vision as soon as I close my eyes. Him at the hotel, holding the drink, watching his jacket fall from my body.

In the hay, braced over me, shirtless, working my body.

Soon he's invading my dreams. I can feel the rope again, tight on my wrist. I smile to myself, reveling in the rush of pleasure and anticipation.

Then something pinches against my skin and I startle awake.

The room is dark.

It shouldn't be dark.

I left the lights on.

I try to move, but I'm immobile. I've been tied. It wasn't a dream.

I can't see anything. The room is pitch black. Even my clock is off.

The electricity has been cut.

"Jax?" I ask, even though I know better.

Silence.

"Colette?" I ask hopefully.

A light flares, the striking of a match.

It moves through the air, illuminating a hand. It rises to a mouth, a cigarette, and a face.

Not Jax's face.

I scream.

14

Jax

We hit a storm over New Mexico. Lightning flashes in the distance and the helicopter jerks and shudders.

"Sorry about the turbulence," the pilot calls back. "Doing my best to avoid the storm but you can't dodge everything."

"That's quite all right," I say. "How far out are we?"

"We're about 50 miles from the heliport, or about 20 minutes," he says.

"At the airport?" I hope this is not the case. Airports mean increased visibility.

"No," Colt says. "It's a private 'port we use. Less paparazzi."

"Good."

Up ahead I can see the lights of Albuquerque glimmering in the dark. Like many US cities in the Southwest, the edges of its sprawl stand in stark contrast to the empty land surrounding it. Particularly at night, when the city streets pulse with streetlights. The late hour means few cars are out, and fewer eyes.

After a few minutes, we move beyond the storm. The chopper swoops low and circles a large landing pad illuminated by bright lights. I can see two black sedans parked beyond the safety perimeter. Their windows are dark but running lights gleam along their edges.

The helicopter sets down with a gentle bump. The pilot powers down the engine, pausing briefly to shake my hand.

I thank Colt.

"Take care of yourself," he says. "Let me know if we can help."

"Will do," I say. I pop open the door and duck

my head against the wash of the helicopter's blades as I climb out.

The door of one sedan opens and a man in a simple dress shirt and slacks climbs out. He stands by the car as I approach, then holds out his hand when I get close.

"Mr. De Luca!" he calls. "The Cure sends his regards." He takes my hand and pumps it with vigor.

"Be sure to pass along my gratitude," I say.

"Of course," says the man and passes over the key fob. "Sorry it's not as fancy as what you're used to."

"It's fine," I reply as I give the sedan a quick onceover. It's a late model Infiniti, an upgraded package from the looks of it. Far from my first choice, but a good one for avoiding undue attention. "Beggars can't be choosers."

The man gives a hearty laugh. "From what I hear, sir, you are about as far from a beggar as one can get."

I climb into the driver's seat. "I'm glad some people still have nice things to say about me." I give the man a quick nod and close the door.

The interior and dash are decidedly lower tech

than I'm used to, almost spartan in comparison to a Vigilante car. But it will do.

"Hello, Infiniti," I try, and am greeted by a helpful chirp as the dash lights up. "Navigate to Nashville, Tennessee."

"Calculating," replies a pleasant female voice. A second later a pale arrow superimposes itself on the windshield. I pull out and follow the car's directions. I note that it has a civilian version of the type of auto-drive you used to only find in Vigilante cars. It's not as sophisticated and is tied to the navigation, but it's something. The Cure gets all the good stuff.

The small heliport is situated too close to downtown for my taste, and I blaze down a narrow street between two tall buildings, the sort I would normally avoid at all cost. Thankfully the Vigilantes don't know where I am.

But I'm only a few blocks down when a car suddenly pulls out of a drive in front of me, blocking the road. I hit the brakes and instinctively check my rearview. A second car has done the same behind me, boxing me in. Damn it. I drove straight into a trap. It's the perfect spot for an ambush maneuver like this.

I have no doubt who is in the cars. With no means of tracking me, the Vigilantes must have guessed I was on one of The Cure's helicopters and simply had to lie in wait to confirm. For all I know, the driver who met me contacted them. I'll have to let The Cure know about this little violation of his protected status.

Once I figure out how to escape this.

15

Mia

No sooner has the scream escaped my lips when I force it to stop.

Don't be a ninny, Mia, I tell myself. Be brave. Face this.

The man stands at the end of my bed, but he's not Jax. He's fair skinned and not quite as tall. He smokes his cigarette. I can only see him when he inhales from it.

"Who are you?" I finally ask.

He leans forward, the cigarette trapped

between his lips. His face is eerily red from the faint light.

He takes the cigarette from his mouth and disappears into the dark again. I follow his hand where the only light is now, by the banister in the corner. He hasn't tied my feet or body, only my wrists.

But it's dark. He can't see me. He's not wearing a night-vision monocle like Jax did that first night.

I think about the ties, touching the turns with my fingertips. Slipknots. Standard issue. My hands are separated, so I can't use the opposite fingers to untie one like I did in the barn. But I remember what Jax said. "Work with the knots."

A slipknot is meant to slide before it locks into place. I just have to move opposite the direction of the turn.

"You didn't answer me," I say, trying to keep my voice steady. I roll my fingers in as far as they will go, trying to pluck at the cross bend in the knot.

"I don't plan to," he says.

His accent is German. Could this be Klaus? The dead Klaus?

Or not-so-dead?

But Klaus was Jax's friend. He wouldn't act like this. I go back to concentrating on my knots.

"What does Jax want with a civilian like you?" he asks.

"What does Jax usually want a woman for?" I fire back.

The man chuckles. "True enough."

Despite my focus on the knot, my belly burns at how everyone assumes I'm some plaything for Jax. I refuse to believe it. Maybe everything I know about dalliances comes from novels, but I'm pretty sure the way we feel is what stories are told about. Not the stuff of beer ads and condom commercials.

I've loosened the knot.

I pause to rest my arm just for a moment. My eyes are starting to adjust to the low light. The man's cigarette drops ash on my bed.

"You're going to start a fire on my grandma's quilt," I say bitterly.

He shakes his head as he takes another drag. His hair is light colored and shaggy.

I start working on the other knot. I can't pull free just yet. This man can't know I can get out of his pathetic ties.

"What did he find so interesting about you?"

he asks. The cigarette comes around to the side of the bed and the mattress dips as he sits next to me.

My skin crawls, but I realize that this is my opportunity to get the upper hand. “Why don’t you come find out?” I say, hoping I sound suggestive. I’m not good at this.

The hand with the cigarette stays by his knee, but another one touches my shoulder. I try not to flinch. The other knot is loose enough for me to go free. I can’t risk that he’ll see me if I let my arm down, so I leave it high.

His hand moves down, tracing the curve of my breast. I steel myself from concerning myself with that and wait for the proper moment.

“Very nice,” he says. “Maybe we need a little illumination so I can see what got Jax so distracted that he made mistakes.”

My throat tightens. What mistakes? Was he caught again?

“You’ve seen him?” I ask, forcing the tremor out of my voice.

“So many questions.” The hand moves over to the buttons of my pajama top and unfastens the first one.

I keep my eye on the cigarette. It’s about to

burn down to his fingers. He'll have to do something about it, and that's when I'll make a move.

Another button comes undone, then another. He moves the fabric aside to brush his fingers across my skin.

Come on, cigarette. Burn.

"Nice," he says.

I decide it's best not to goad him or talk, but just wait. Goose bumps pop on my skin from the chill, but I'm definitely not moved by this man. I'm pleased to know that it really was Jax, and that I haven't become some BDSM love-slave addict.

He finally notices the cigarette and pauses to stab it out on my antique side table.

Asshole!

I jerk my arms from the ropes and pull them to me in one fast move. Before he can totally extinguish the light, I have a timber-hitch tie around his wrist.

He moves back in surprise, but I've already locked it down. I use the banister as a pulley to drag him forward and his head cracks against the table.

"That's for damaging a one-hundred-year-old table," I tell him.

I snag his free hand and whip a fast rolling hitch around it. Two different knots to confuse him if he gets one undone.

I can't see a thing now that the cigarette is out, but he's decently tied with both hands immobilized. Still, I have to assume he's Vigilante and is trained to escape.

Since I don't have any ends to work with, only the middle, I go with a clove hitch to secure this jerk to my banister. I jump onto the bed, feeling my way up the pole, and pull the tie down over it. I know this is a knot that can be undone if your hands are free, but luckily, Pale Boy's aren't.

"I like to get a little freaky," I tell him as I feel along his body. "Hope you don't mind."

He doesn't answer, and I know he's probably got some tech on him that can get him help. For all I know he can use brain waves to send a message.

I have to get out of here.

His pockets are full of lumps. I pull everything out that I can find, take off his watch, and just for fun, pull his pants down around his ankles.

And, because I know the power of shoes, I take those too.

I've piled everything on the bed. I extract what

I think are car keys and drop them in the little sewn pocket on my top. Since I can't see what I'm doing, I twist the quilt into a loose bundle. I gather it up and back away from the room until I'm in the hall.

And run.

Through the house, fighting the front door locks, and out onto the porch into the pale moonlight. I don't see this man's car anywhere. Damn it. I'll just take my own.

I dash back into the house, snatch my keys, and race across the yard.

The old Ford growls to life. I back out of the drive, now wishing I'd thought to grab some of the tech from the pantry stash. Doesn't matter. I don't know how to use it.

I'm at the end of the driveway when I realize — I have nowhere to go. What should I do?

Damn.

I scan the fields. Did someone just drop this guy off? I pull out and ease along the deserted road.

And I see it.

A car, about two hundred yards away.

I pull up behind it and drag the stolen key chain from my pocket. If it's like Jax's, it will — yes, as soon as I approach, the keyless locks pop right up.

I drag the door open and squeal a little. It's a Vigilante-tech car, just like Colette's and Jax's.

Do I dare drive it?

I sit in the seat. Once my weight hits the cushion, the car engine fires up, low and rumbling.

I scramble back to my Ford and grab the quilt full of stolen goods. I dump it in the passenger seat and look out the front windshield.

Holy crap, I'm stealing a car and heading into danger.

I give out a whoop and shove the gearshift into drive.

16

Jax

I crouch low in The Cure's Infiniti. Blasted civilian windows and their transparency. If the Vigilantes follow standard procedure, they'll either attempt a knockout shot through a window, or simply throw a stun grenade. A full firefight is usually out of the question in normal city streets, but with the kill order, they might be willing to clean up a mess.

Regardless, staying here is not an option.

The car blocking the front of me is perfectly

positioned between brick buildings. I can't get around it.

I flick on the car's rear camera. I have better luck there, since the second car stopped close to the corner.

The sedan behind me is positioned as well as it can be in the space between a stop sign and a building. But there is a gap behind it just large enough for me to fit through. If I try to shoot for the rear gap, they can close it off easily. But then that leaves the pole side open.

Using the backup camera to navigate in the dark, I throw the car in reverse and floor it, angling toward the gap behind the Vigilante car. As I suspected, the other car reverses to close off the gap. I shove the gear back into drive and send the Infiniti lurching to the opposite side. It jumps the curb and plows into the stop sign.

"Sorry, Cure," I mutter, wincing at the damage to the car.

The Vigilante realizes his mistake and tries to block off my new avenue. I brace myself and feel the car shudder as it takes a hit in the side. But I floor it and break away, taking out some bricks on the corner of the building.

Now both Vigilantes are behind me.

I can hear a fender scraping a tire. I'll need to ditch this Infiniti. It's not cut out for this level of abuse.

I could really use one of the Vigilante vehicles. I have to lure one of them out.

I bark a command at the car and the navigation shifts to an overhead map. I cancel the route before the car starts giving me new directions and study the street layout as best I can. The longer I drive, the more chances they get to cut me off, and they won't fall for the same trick again. Not to mention attracting the attention of law enforcement as we roar through the streets.

Pulling over to ditch the car won't work. They can track me via thermal imagery once I'm out of the vehicle. There's not exactly any rivers to duck into here. I need something else.

In the rearview mirror I see a car careen around a corner and swing in behind me. The damaged fender tells me it's the Vigilante that failed to cut off my escape. The Infiniti has plenty of horsepower but I hold no illusions as to how it would fare against a Vigilante sedan.

I yank the wheel hard and slide around a

corner. My pursuer overshoots and swings wide, buying me a few precious seconds over him. I zigzag between streets, mindful of the silent countdown before the local police show up. At least at this hour the streets are mostly empty. The last thing I need is to get yet another civilian involved in my mess.

Up ahead of me a car turns onto the street. Damn it, the second Vigilante is ahead and barreling straight for me. Who is driving that car? They're rivaling Colette in ability. Has to be another Phase Six.

I make a last-second hard right and barely avoid sideswiping a garbage truck rumbling the opposite way. This won't work much longer.

A cloud of white smoke billows out from behind an industrial complex up ahead, and the germ of an idea forms. I pull another hard right and spot what I'm looking for. Three large condensers line up against a building, each belching out clouds of steam. The facility is lit up like a football field.

I can't let them follow my heat signature even for a second. I roll down the window as the condensers approach. The third is the lowest but it's still a hell of a jump.

I run the Infiniti as close to the wall as I can. I turn on the navigator and set the auto-drive to go straight ahead and come to a halt in 1000 feet. I roll down the window. I've only got one shot at this. If I miss, they'll pick me up.

We approach the steam of the condensers. Here we go.

I climb up through the window, pass the first condenser, then the second, so close that my shoulder rubs the wall. When we get to the third, I launch from the car and into the steam, not really certain what will be there when I land.

I crash onto the metal roof and stop just short of the grate.

The surface is flat and hot. I jump to my knees, move to the edge, and peer through the steam.

The heat prickles my skin and the moisture dampens my hair, but I should have some cover, both visual and thermal. I watch as the first Vigilante car, the one with the damaged fender, follows the Infiniti as it rolls to a stop. The second car passes, but doesn't follow the first. That Vigilante knows I'm not in there. He'll keep looking.

From the first car emerges a figure clad in a

familiar outfit. I stifle a laugh.

It's the cocky guard from the silo I visited with Mia. Running Man, in his close-fitting running clothes.

Oh, I'm going to enjoy this.

He moves to the Infiniti, a weapon in his hand. On his head he has some sort of monocle, probably a night-vision lens. Cautiously he sweeps the car before yanking the door open, weapon ready. When I don't jump out at him, he looks around. His gaze moves up to the top of the condensers, but through the mist I can't tell if he's spotted me.

He heads my way. His pace is unhurried, and his gaze is everywhere. He's still looking.

He moves around to the back of the condenser next to mine. I strain for the sound of feet on the metal ladder above the constant hiss of the condensers, but hear nothing. Carefully I shift position and spot him, still circling the condenser down below. He's between them now, staring at the soft earth instead of looking up. An apparent and futile attempt at looking for tracks, I wager.

I don't hesitate. With a quick roll I'm off the roof and hurtling for his head. I slam into him with both feet, knocking us both to the ground. I roll as I land and am back on my feet before he's even looking around. I aim a sharp kick at his jaw and send him sprawling back, then leap on him and wrap him in a choke hold.

His hands finally find some purchase and he digs fingers like iron bars into my bicep. I feel part of my arm go numb and my hold loosens. He twists in my grip, his hand scrabbling for a better angle.

I drop the hold and lash out with my other arm, cracking his head to the side. Then I dig my own fingers into his flesh, hunting for a bundle of nerves. He fights for a second, then goes limp.

I waste no time. That move can drop a normal person for several minutes, but a Vigilante's training greatly reduces its effectiveness. I snag his control watch and key fob, then run back to his car. The door opens at my approach and I dive in.

I resist the urge to floor it in case the other Vigilante car is nearby, and instead make a quick yet graceful U-turn on the street. With a second turn the condensers are out of sight, their great steam clouds still billowing above the neighboring buildings.

"Computer," I bark, "cloaking levels one, two, and three."

"Cloaking levels initiated."

I relax a little into the seat. I have no idea what kind of authorizations Running Man has, but I suspect they're not very high. This will hide me from his partner, but the Vigilantes themselves will be able to track this car before long.

I drive over a gully and slow down long enough to roll down the window and toss Running Man's gear out. The car scolds me for compromising the cloaking, but quiets down once the window is closed. That will buy me a little more time. Hopefully enough for this next step.

"Computer, deactivate cloaking level two. Send secure transmission to Operative 03773." Hopefully Sam can handle a message from me without complications.

Sam comes on the screen full of seriousness. "What fuckup have you done this time, Paulson?" Then he sees me and cracks a smile. "You son of a gun. Did you take out Paulson?"

"Is that his name?" I say. "He needs to be relegated to kitchen duty."

"One of Carter's boys in Missouri," Sam says. "I'm guessing he fouled up your apprehension."

"In a big way. Not sure what happened to the

other. Slick driver."

"You know her well," Sam says.

"Seriously?" I should have recognized Colette's driving. "She going to end up on the rack because of me?"

"Nah. She's playing by the book. She's good." He glances down and frowns. "Let me wipe this car before they figure out it's you."

The dash goes dark and everything electronic in the car goes out. The engine continues its quiet hum. I've left the streets of downtown Albuquerque and am heading toward the desert.

The system reboots and Sam comes back on. "I'll be in touch as I can. I have to cover these tracks." He kills the transmission.

Time for me to head back to Tennessee and see if Jovana is stupid enough to attend that fight.

And tell The Cure about the unfortunate state of his Infiniti.

17

MIA

Holy crap, this car. I feel like Jax!

The accelerator moves almost on its own, as if it can sense when I want to speed up or slow down. I'm distracted by the screen in the dash and the displays on the windshield. When I run off the road for the third time in five minutes, a sultry female voice from the speakers asks, "Would you like to commence auto-drive?"

I wonder what that entails. Is it like cruise control, where it manages your speed? Jax sometimes turned all the way around in his car, paying no attention to the steering wheel.

"Yes," I say.

But as soon as my voice is registered, the voice says, "Authentication needed."

I don't see or hear anything scanning me, but I sense I'm being monitored.

"Pulse rate elevated," the voice says. "Heat signature not in database."

The car starts to slow down. I push on the accelerator, but nothing happens.

Crap!

"I'm Mia Morrow," I say quickly, then add, "A special."

I'm trying to impress a car.

"Mia Morrow verified." The car begins to speed up again. "Auto-drive initiated."

The wheel starts to move beneath my hands. It neatly manages a curve.

We pass a speed limit sign and the voice says, "Please state your preferences for our records. Speed limit? Below or above? Provide your answer in five-mile-per-hour increments."

"Speed limit," I say. The car slows down to precisely sixty-five miles per hour.

Well, that's boring. "Actually," I add, "one hundred miles per hour over the speed limit."

The car shoots forward like a rocket. A visible beam shoots out ahead of the car, following the white line to guide its direction.

I clutch at the wheel, but the movements are disconcerting, so I let go again and grip my seat belt, which has tightened down against me.

"Destination?" the car asks.

"Uh, actually, let's do the speed limit," I say.

The car glides to a normal speed. The light beam goes out, although the steering wheel continues to follow the curve of the road. I guess it takes bonus tech to auto-drive at high speeds.

"Destination?" the voice asks again.

I don't know what to tell it. "Jax De Luca?" I ask.

"Whereabouts unknown," it says. "Last known location: Ridley Prison. Would you like to go to Ridley Prison?"

"No," I say quickly. Weird it doesn't know Jax was at a silo a few days ago. But I definitely don't want to go to the jail. For all I know the car will bust through the walls. I think for a second. "Colette," I say. Shoot, I don't know her last name.

"There are 17,576 women with the name Colette in the mainland USA," the voice says. "Please narrow your choices."

"Colette the Vigilante," I say.

"Mia Morrow is not authorized for that information," the voice says.

Well, boo.

I can't go to a silo. I can't get to Jax or Colette.

The road is quiet. Only the occasional car passes, its headlights piercing the dark.

"Destination?" the car insists.

I'm beginning to hate her. "Stop auto-drive," I say. Maybe now she'll leave me alone.

I hold on to the wheel again. I'm probably a sitting duck in this car. As soon as Klaus gets free, he'll alert someone. He might even be able to take control of his vehicle remotely.

What was I thinking?

Still, the giddiness of being in such a car doesn't fade.

"Does this car have a stealth mode?" I ask.

"This Aston Martin is equipped with three cloaking levels," it says. "One. Heat and infrared. Two. Radar and transmissions. Three. Low visibility."

"I want them all," I say.

"Reminders. All internal heating will be turned off. All ability to communicate will be cut. Low visibility can only be achieved in certain light levels and environments."

"Fine, fine," I say. "Just do it."

"Cloaking levels one, two, and three initiated," it says.

I try to relax. I figure Pale Boy and whoever sent him will think I'm clueless. Hopefully this car is smarter than they are.

I drive for another hour, fighting sleep. I don't know where I'm headed or what I'm doing next. When I feel like I've done enough random zigzagging on highways and back roads to make it difficult to figure out my path, I pull over beside a twenty-four-hour convenience store to look at my stash.

"Can I get a light?" I ask the car.

"Interior lights will compromise cloaking levels one and three."

"That's fine," I say. "It's just for a minute."

An overhead light pops on.

The sight of my grandma's quilt gives me some comfort in the unfamiliar car. I'm glad I took it. I don't know if I'll ever get home again.

The pile of gadgets I took doesn't mean anything to me. The watch, the shoes, bits of metal with no obvious use. Two slender metal wands. The big onyx ring I was wearing is in there. It must have fallen off my finger during the struggle. I put it on again.

I sit back against the driver's seat. What am I doing here? Nobody knows where Jax is. This car won't help me.

Maybe I should just drive to the silo and take my chances.

"Your temperature and pulse indicate fatigue and hunger," the car says. "Would you like a cold beverage or caffeine shot?"

"Yes to the cold beverage," I say. Good thing, since I don't have a penny to my name to even walk into the convenience store.

A list of drinks scrolls on the dashboard screen. I choose "Mr. Pibb" and have to smile that my would-be abductor has the same soft-drink preferences as me.

A buzzing sound by my elbow makes me shift nearer the door. The console opens and a can of Mr. Pibb rises from inside.

This, I understand. I take the can. Can Vigilantes get anything they want, anytime they want it? I remember Jax calling that guy to bring me clothes. Who was that? Armond? I had been half asleep, but I caught the end of the conversation.

Armond. Could he find Jax for me?

If this is Klaus's car, he would know Armond too. And Armond isn't a Vigilante, so it shouldn't snub me.

"I need to contact someone," I tell the car.

"This will compromise cloaking level two," the voice says.

"Fine. Whatever. Please contact Armond," I say. Then I realize, shoot, I don't know his last name either.

"There are 1,598 men with the name Armond in the mainland USA—"

"The one who designs Jax's suits."

"Contact found. Would you like a secure transmission?"

My heart speeds up. "Yes," I say.

"Connecting."

It's going to do it!

After a moment, the bald man I remember from before comes onscreen. "Identify yourself," he barks. Then his face softens when he sees me. “Who are you?” he asks.

“I’m a friend of Jax,” I say quickly. “The girl he got the clothes for.”

Armond frowns. “I’ve made a lot of women’s clothes —”

“Recently,” I say. I don’t want to know about all the clothes Jax has commissioned for other women. “In St. Louis. The red sweater dress and blue pantsuit.”

“Ah, yes,” he says, sitting back. “*Que bonita*, very slight. Did you like the clothes? Jax favors the color red.”

“I noticed,” I say. “I need to find him.”

Armond laughs. “Many a pretty lady has tried to locate the elusive Jax.”

My face burns hot. “Not like that. I — I stole a car for him.”

Armond sobers and looks around me. “Who’s had this car?”

“I don’t know. A man came and tied me up. I got free. Jax would want to know.”

“What sort of man?” Armond asks.

“Pale. German accent.”

“*Dios*,” Armond says. “This is interesting.”

"Can you find him for me? Or at least get him a message?"

"I can try," he says.

"Tell him the safe house was compromised again. A man, slightly shorter than Jax, pale, blond, with a German accent. He wanted to know why Jax was interested in me."

"Are you safe?" Armond's bushy eyebrows draw together in concern.

"I don't know," I say, trying to force a laugh. "I did steal this car!"

"Do you know how to use it?"

"I'm figuring it out. I have it cloaked."

He nods. "Good, good." He glances down. "You sent this securely. Do you want to unencrypt it so I can send Jax your location?"

Unease flows through me. "No. Just tell him to meet me —" I try to think. What sort of code could I use about where to go?

A map is projected on the screen. I'm in a small town called Jamestown. But I'm just twenty miles from one named Alpine.

"Tell Jax I learned how to tie an alpine coil in Tennessee," I say.

"All right," Armond says. "I will try. Be

careful, my dear."

"I will."

The screen reverts to its standard line of commands.

I can only hope Jax isn't too far away.

18

Jax

I'm just inside the Tennessee state line when Sam patches through on an encrypted channel.

"Don't tell me. You need a cinnamon roll," I say.

Sam doesn't laugh.

"This'll be quick since I have to cover my tracks," he says. "You need to head to Alpine, Tennessee. Pronto. Mia is waiting for you."

"What? Mia?" My hackles rise.

"She was attacked at the safe house by a man

with a German accent."

"Klaus?"

Sam nods. "Possibly. Apparently she tied him up. She also stole an Aston Martin from the guy."

"My car?"

"That's what Armond says. He got a visual during the transmission. When Mia couldn't find you, she contacted him. Smart lady. Okay, I'm out. Get to her, Jax. They're on to her."

He kills the transmission.

Holy hell. Mia is in the game.

This is an incredible betrayal by Klaus.

My fury is hard to contain that someone who once worked so closely with me is now in league with Jovana. If I hadn't seen all the evidence myself, I would never have believed it.

There's something larger at play here. More than Jovana getting me out of the way to protect her father's criminal network. My mistake in killing Singer for her is part of a bigger plot. I aim to find out what it is, but not until I know Mia is secure.

I'm doing a shit job convincing myself I only care about her safety. I haven't stopped thinking about her since she took off down that drive back in Missouri.

But I was right to let her go then.

Just like it's right to meet up with her now.

It's eighty-five miles from where I am to Alpine, which is more of a community than a town. I probably shouldn't call attention to myself, but now that Sam has wiped this car, I decide, screw it, and plug into semi-stealth at high speeds. Without Vigilante status, I don't have the luxury of blatantly ignoring civilian safety laws, but this car can repel standard-issue speed monitoring easily enough.

Mia has shown more pluck than I gave her credit for. Tying up a Vigilante and stealing his car? Who does that? As a silo director, I rarely saw trainees come through with that level of tenacity. Hell, I rarely saw full-fledged Vigilantes take that level of risk.

Other than my team. Sam. Colette. And back in the day, Klaus.

If I have his car, I can get to Jovana for sure. The data inside it will lead me directly to her. His driving history. The identities of people who rode in it.

I want that car. It used to be mine, until I got sent to Ridley. Klaus kept it.

Supposedly for me.

As the car hurtles along the freeway, I keep telling myself this is why I'm headed Mia's way. My car.

The town is in the middle of nowhere. Population 496. It's the middle of the night now and hardly anything but freight trucks are on the road.

The Aston Martin should be easy to spot.

The town is silent and still as a morgue. I cruise along the highway and pull up to the blinking red light. Mia sure chose a fitting location. She's a country girl through and through.

Ahead is a convenience store, probably the only establishment in the whole town that's open. I scan for my car, but the only vehicle in the crumbling parking lot is a battered Volvo.

Where is she?

I pass by a string of storefronts on what might once have been a bustling square. Just on the other side I see another building with the lights on. A diner. I glance at the clock on the dash. 2 a.m. Must be an all-nighter for truck drivers. Two big rigs are taking up a line of parking spots.

I roll past them and there it is, my sleek little silver Aston Martin. Klaus better not have put a scratch on it.

The diner has broad windows showing the interior. Difficult to defend. But a quick glance tells me Mia isn't inside. You can see every booth and stool.

I pull up next to the car. Satisfaction courses through me just looking at it. She will be mine again.

It, I correct myself. The car.

Not the girl.

I walk up to it. The windows are fitted with false blackout screens that make it appear you can see inside even though you can't. I tap on the glass, knowing I am breaking the security grid.

I can't see the red alarm or hear the warning, but the door flies open and Mia shoots out of the car like an arrow.

She stares at it a minute like it's possessed. She wears flannel pajamas and a pair of men's shoes that are way too large for her. I have to squelch the urge to take her in my arms. She looks lost and frightened.

"Sorry," I say.

She freezes, stands up straight, and touches her wild loose hair before she turns around.

Her face is calm now. "Jax," she says. "You

came." Either she's hiding her emotions or it's no big thing to her that I showed up.

I'm not sure what sort of welcome I expected. Hysterics, I suppose. Throwing herself at me. She had been so insistent that I keep her before.

I stuff down any disappointment at her nonchalance. "You called."

"The car is yelling at me," she says.

This makes me laugh. "I set off the alarm."

"Oh." Her shoulders relax. "I thought I'd broken something."

"What were you doing?"

She lifts her arm and shows me a Vigilante watch a lot like the one that was confiscated from me at the silo. "I was punching all the buttons."

I take the watch off her wrist. "Do you always act this impulsively?"

Her eyes flick to the ground. "I had nothing to do while I waited for you, and no idea how long you'd be. You didn't contact me."

"You had the car in stealth. You couldn't receive transmissions."

"Oh."

I lean inside the car with the watch and press the all-clear. The interior light stops pulsing and the feminine voice silences its concerned intonations.

"It's a nice car," she says.

"It used to be mine."

"Really?" She glances back at it. "I like it."

Too many of the buttons on her pajama top are undone and my groin tightens. "Aren't you cold?" I ask. "You always seem to be out in your sleepwear.'"

She glances down, notices the buttons, and frantically begins to fasten them. "I didn't exactly have time to change after I escaped from that man in my bedroom."

My eyebrows shoot up. "Bedroom?" Sam hadn't mentioned this.

Her cheeks bloom pink. "He tied me to the posts like you did. Are all Vigilantes this kinky?"

My gaze slides down to the top, now buttoned to the neck. I imagine Klaus unfastening them and a rage burns in my belly. "What else did Klaus do?"

Her face changes. "Klaus? So he isn't dead."

"The reports of his demise were greatly exaggerated." I take her arm and drag her to the other side of the Aston Martin. "Get in," I say and open her door.

She ducks inside, scooting aside a quilt filled

with all sorts of Vigilante tech. "Where did you get that?" I ask.

Her face beams up at me, all innocence. "I stole it."

Picturing her rooting through Klaus's clothes on the floor beside her bed sends another shot of fury through me. I slam the door and go around to the driver's side.

I take a few seconds to restore my driving status in the computer and relegate Klaus to a guest driver so I can retain his data. Then we jet out of the parking lot.

"Where are we going?" Mia asks. She's bubbly and exuberant, like we're on some sort of vacation jaunt.

I spot a motel ahead. The office is dark. That's fine. I don't need their pathetic keys. I've got Mia back under my protection and I will not allow Klaus or anyone else to do anything to her.

The car banks hard to the right as I jerk the wheel to circle around to the back side of the building. There were only two cars out front, and back here, there are none.

"Here?" she asks. I hear a small tremor in her voice.

I stop the car. My break-in kit is tucked in the door pocket just like I left it a year ago.

The back side of the motel has four rooms. I choose the second door. It's locked with a simple deadbolt that I open with a strong magnet as if I were flipping it by hand on the other side.

Mia jumps out of the car, all energy and excitement. "Is this where we're going to make a plan?" She looks around. "Are Sam and Colette coming? Have you ridden in her car? It goes over water!"

The door isn't closed more than a second when I snatch her hand and jerk her toward me. "Shut up, Mia," I say. And before I can contemplate my next move myself, I've pulled her into me and my lips are crushing hers.

19

MIA

Jax has completely stolen my breath.

I clutch at his shirt, unbuttoned at the throat. His lips roam over mine. The stubble on his jaw is rough against my skin.

His hands are on my waist, holding me against him. He smells of the outdoors, pine trees and cut wood.

His chest is solid. He bends down to me, his mouth hot and demanding. I'm spinning, the ground shifting beneath my feet. I sway against him and his arms wrap around my body. His belt buckle presses against my belly, and below that, I feel him, thick and hard.

We're alone. In a motel.

And he's kissing me.

Oh my God.

My breath comes in a great gasp, and Jax pulls away. His face looms over mine, a lock of hair falling over his forehead. The room is dark, only a nightlight by the bed providing the faintest glow. I can't see his eyes, only the dim planes of his face. He looks angry. Intense. Like a monster in the dark.

But I'm not afraid.

He tries to pull away, but I snake my arms around him and hold fast.

"I won't take advantage of your innocence," he says.

"You're not," I tell him.

Now he's even angrier. "Did Klaus do the job, then?"

I don't know what he's asking. "What job?" I ask.

He shakes his head slowly. "How can you be so seductive and so naive at the same time?" His voice cuts me with its anger and coldness.

I let go of him. “I never understand you.” I walk over to the corner of the bed and sit down, feeling defeated and lost. “You pull me close. You push me away.”

My heart still pounds like a frightened rabbit. I touch my lips, hot and swollen. And my cheek, tender from his stubble. I don’t feel adventurous and strong anymore. I’m like a little girl, scolded by a parent.

The bed is elaborate, with a roof and curtains pulled back with a sash. I lie on my side and pull my knees up to my chest. “Take your stupid car,” I say. “Just leave me here. I’ll figure something out.” I can go back to community college. Abandon the house. Let the town have it. I don’t care.

Find some normal boy. Somebody like that grocery sacker, calm and easy. No hooded eyes and spy gadgets and secure silos and jumping into rivers. No stripping me and drinking Old Fashioneds and having women dress me in red lingerie.

No ropes.

Actually, maybe I’ll keep the ropes.

Jax hasn’t moved, or at least I assume he hasn’t. My eyes are squeezed closed and the room is dark anyway. I haven’t heard his footsteps.

"Mia," he says. His voice is different now. Instead of cold, it's like the rumble of a race car, low and powerful.

I don't answer. I can't manage his crazy moods. "You're worse than a girl," I say, not caring anymore if I make him mad. "Changing your mind all the time."

I don't hear a sound, but I know he's moved close. His body gives off heat even though we have no contact.

Every part of my body senses his nearness. It's like I'm humming from the inside out, vibrating, anticipating. I lie very, very still so I don't accidentally touch him with my own movement.

The first thing that shifts is my hair. He's brushing it away from my face, his touch as light as air. My scalp tingles. Then his fingertips caress my cheek.

I hold my breath again. We only connect in this barest of contacts, but somehow, my entire body responds. A swirl of tension starts to form low in my belly.

"Breathe, Mia," he whispers. His face is much closer than I expected. I can feel his words whisper against my forehead.

Then his lips are there, pressed against my skin. A hand on my shoulder guides me so that I roll onto my back.

"I just want to see you again," he says.

I hear a click and a light illuminates his face. He's holding some sort of flat device that is as bright as the moon. He sets it on the table beside the bed. Now one side of us is softly lit, and the other falls to darkness.

I want to ask him if he's going to tie me up, if that's what he likes. But my throat is tight and dry. This isn't going to stop, I can tell, and a tendril of fear slips through me. Not at what we'll do, or if it will hurt. But that I will be a disappointment to him, and then he will send me away again.

"Do you have the rope?" I ask him. This is one place where I feel confident that I can stand apart from the untold numbers of women he has certainly taken to bed. I glance up at the curtains pulled back on the bed. There is a sash.

His eyebrow lifts and he suppresses a smile a little too late for me to not notice it. "Is that what you like?"

"I don't know." I hesitate. "I liked what we did before. In the barn."

He watches me a moment. "There will be time for that, for ropes." His fingers pluck at the first button on my pajamas. "Tonight is for discovery."

The air is cool on my skin as he works his way down, the flannel top falling open as he goes. He's seen me so many times. I don't feel any shyness as he slips the fabric across my breasts and exposes them to his gaze.

My nipples tighten in the chill. One of his hands cups a breast, his thumb teasing the tip. He lowers his face to mine again, his mouth hot and insistent. I relax against the mattress, my tongue tentatively searching for his. All the emotions swirl together. Nervousness. Excitement. Urgency.

Jax braces on an elbow over me and lowers his body onto mine. He is solid and muscled. The weight is welcome, and all on their own, my knees come up around him on either side.

He sucks in a breath and trails his mouth down my neck, across my collarbone, and up the rise of a breast. When he captures a nipple, my body responds wildly, arching up to him. Now I'm swamped with one singular feeling — need.

I know what happens between couples. I wrote about it to Jax in our letters. Now he's here, and I'm frustrated by the clothes, caught in the demands of my body.

Jax understands my sudden desperation and feeds it by yanking the shirt off my shoulders. He lifts me and the pajama top is gone, hitting the floor next to the bed. The onyx ring, loose on my finger, comes off and goes with it, but I let it go.

I feel bold and reach for his waist, tugging his crisp shirt from his belt. Then it is my turn with the buttons, my fingers fumbling as Jax makes his way across my shoulder and into my neck with his mouth.

We're going to do this. I'm going to do this. My brain is still processing where we are, what is happening. I don't know if Jax will like it, or if he'll ever want me again after he gets it, but I decide then and there that I don't care. One night with him is worth the grief that might follow. I'll take it.

I'll try to be worth the trouble I've caused him.

His shirt opens and I run my hands up the solid plank of his abs and to his taut chest. I can't take his shirt off while he's braced on his elbows, but his mouth is back down low and my mind goes blank as he takes a nipple in his mouth and draws it deeply in.

One of his hands moves to my waist, and my nerves do a small jangle in my head when a finger slips inside the elastic band of my pajamas. I'm on fire, the urgency licking at me, but I don't know what to expect or when it will hurt. He touched me before, and it was fine. But this time it will go so much further.

Jax must feel my subtle shift into tension because he lifts his head. "I'll be careful," he says.

I want to weep, washed over with tenderness and something else, something touching and warm, tingly in a different way from what I feel when he touches me.

But he eases the soft pants over my hips and the fire takes over again. He gives a little growl and shifts his weight.

My legs go flat down on the bed again as he moves off me enough to yank my pants to my knees in one swift jerk.

The oversized shoes I stole from Klaus kick off easily. Jax leans over me, his hands moving across my belly. I wish I had the red thong again, or something pretty, but I'm back to my plain white underwear.

"I'm beginning to really like this look," Jax

says, his thumbs slipping inside the elastic of the legs.

I can barely breathe again, waiting for him to touch me where I want him to go.

"Are you cold?" he asks.

I shake my head no. I don't trust my voice now.

"So beautiful," he whispers. His hand travels up from my hip, over my ribs, along the swell of a breast and back up to my jaw. "I could look at this all night."

His mouth meets mine again, and this kiss is careful, measured, under tight control. I start to feel that he wants to unleash, but he's holding back, for my sake.

I'm grateful. Everything is so full of sensation, so overwhelming, that I have to work through each part on its own.

His chest is on mine now, skin to skin, and I wrap my arms around him, holding him against me. I've never touched so much of another person or had so much contact.

Jax shifts over again, letting his hand trail down my body. I know where he's going this time, and my hips thrust upward to meet him. He touches me outside the panties, and my legs part without my telling them to. His fingers slide up along the folds and press hard against the nub.

Even through the cotton fabric, his touch sends sensations spiraling through me, pleasure, need, desire. I clutch at his strong arm and let myself fall into it, as though there is some vast collection of stars I will hurtle through.

Jax slips a finger inside the panties and my entire body responds. I suck in air against his mouth. It's even more intense than in the barn, without the distraction of the task of untying the knots and the rough hay beneath us.

Something begins to build, and I can't think of anything else but this tight intense feeling brought out by his touch. My hips begin to roll all on their own, working with his movements.

Jax fights the panties a moment more, then rips them down with an impatient growl. His mouth leaves mine and he kneels over me, spreading my knees. He looks like a warrior, muscled and tense, his eyes dark gray.

Then he leans and his lips meet my belly, leaving a damp trail as he moves down. When his mouth finds its destination, my hips lurch up to him.

I can't breathe again, caught in the rapture of his attention, suckling the nub, then his tongue spearing into my body.

His strong hands hold fast to my thighs, pressing them wide as he dives in. I clutch at the bedspread, long since lost, the stars showering down on me now. The spiraling sensation intensifies, and the tight powerful urgency reaches a fever pitch. Everything holds still just for a moment, this pleasure, his careful, insistent movements, and then it all just lets go.

A cry escapes as my body ripples with intensity, the cascades pulsing through me. I'm overwhelmed by it and hold Jax's head, letting the sensations wash over me, waves that keep coming, tight and strong.

Then I fall back and everything drifts down. Jax moves gently below, drawing out the gentle ripples that slowly even out into a soft contentment.

I want to weep, to collapse into emotion. I'm overwhelmed by how I feel about Jax, but I know I can't succumb to that. I've read books. I know better. Women always mix up gratitude, sex, and love. I won't do it.

I open my eyes. Jax watches me quietly, his

eyes less intense now. "You all right?" he asks.

As content as I feel, I want to know the rest of it, what happens next. "I am," I tell him. "But it's time for you to lose those pants."

20

Jax

Mia doesn't have to say that twice. I push away from the bed and shuck off my shoes as I unbuckle my belt. Mia is responsive and sensitive. Watching her orgasm never gets old.

But I know what lies ahead. I unzip my pants and watch her with unwavering attention. If she hesitates, I will drop back. Hold off. If I can.

Her eyes are not shy about following my boxers as they hit the floor. She has a quiet curiosity about her that threatens the tenuous control I'm barely hanging on to as it is.

She gets up on her knees and holds out her hands. I kick away the clothes and move closer to the bed.

Her hands want to explore me and it will be hard to just stand there and let her. She squeezes my shoulders and follows my arms to my elbows. Then across my belly and up my chest. I hold still, allowing her to take her time.

She glances down and takes her first timid hold on my erection. My jaw tics, fighting the urge to push her back on the bed and slam into her. The reach makes her breasts squeeze together into a tantalizing display. I reach out and slide a finger between them. Her breath catches.

Mia squeezes me and slides along the length. I clamp down all the raging desires and continue to trace lazy patterns across her body.

She concentrates on her task, moving more quickly but keeping her grip. I hold on to her shoulders a moment, working the control, but the year in prison is weighing on me now and I've thought of this moment too many times to hold back any longer. I have to be careful with her, and in one more minute, I won't be able to.

I press her back on the bed. She lets go of me and leans against the pillows, eyes wide.

I tug the bedspread away so the sheets are beneath us. Mia's face is less calm than it was before, her eyes filled with worry.

I plan to tell her, "We don't have to do this," and the words are on my lips. But my body isn't going to obey, and I'm already settling over her. I settle for "It will be okay," and a light kiss against her cheek.

"Do we need protection?" she asks.

"Reversible vasectomies are standard issue for male Vigilantes," I tell her. "But if you'd like something for safety reasons, I'm equipped."

She shakes her head. "No, I want to know what this feels like."

Her arms come around my back in a vise grip. I brush the hair off her face. I know I need to get her a little more ready for this. She can't be tense. I lower my mouth to that succulent breast and tease her nipple.

Then my hand goes down low where she is still wet and warm. I circle the hard little nub until she starts to relax, warm and supple below me again.

With as much subtlety as I can manage, I shift

over her, keeping my hand in place. Her knees go around me again, and her eyes are closed.

She tenses a little when I first fit myself inside, but I just work the edges and she calms again.

I feel it when I bump against the barrier. It gives a little, but still resists. Mia's brows draw together, and I know she senses this is about to happen. Her eyes are closed in concentration.

I lean down to kiss her until her lips are soft and pliant and she isn't thinking about her concerns.

Then I swiftly press hard inside.

She gasps against me, every muscle tensing. I hold still a second. Gradually her body goes soft. "You all right?" I ask.

She nods.

I move against her and she stiffens again, but not as much this time. I'm raging with the need to plunge into her, but I hold myself carefully in check.

I reach down for her and work her body. She lets out a soft sigh and her knees fall loose.

Still, I am careful and slow. I find a second well of control and hold tight to it, watching her as I move. I keep going, easing as gently as I can.

Mia opens her eyes. "I won't break," she says and moves to the edge of the bed.

I adjust with her. She reaches between us to touch me near where we're joined. The intensity spikes, and I'm out of the control zone.

"I was thinking something more like this," she says, and suddenly the tables are turned. We're rolling on the bed, and before I know what she's done, she has a satin sash around my wrists.

"Impressive," I say, intending to jerk right out of her ties and take her hard. But then I realize I can't.

I glance up at what she's done. She's lashing the length of the satin cord around the metal frame of the bed. Probably I could yank hard enough and dent the rod.

But now I'm curious what she's up to.

Her hands roll down my chest. "You were being a little too gentle," she says.

And straddles me.

I'm raging now. She lifts herself up and slips me inside. I've never allowed a woman to tie me. But I let her.

Then my brain is erased as she starts to move. For someone who's never done this before, she's managed to master the pace.

"I want to feel it," she whispers, and I know

what she means.

Still, I manage to hold on, reveling in the sensation of her sliding up and down my length. Her breasts sway slightly and her brown-gold hair falls over her shoulders. I want to touch her, but can't provide any brain energy to undoing her knots. Besides, I have a feeling she's learned fast and it won't be as easy as it was in the car.

She leans forward, her nipples brushing against my chest. "What makes Jax lose control?" she whispers. Her hands move up my rib cage to settle on either side of my face. She grinds down hard, our bodies tight against each other.

Pretty much this, I want to say, and the urgency breaks into an explosion.

Mia holds on as I pulse into her. Jesus. It's been forever. And this girl. This crazy innocent unexpected woman.

She looks down at me with a pleased expression. "That was amazing!" she says and almost suppresses a giggle. "Can we do it again?"

"Not immediately," I say, her laugh infecting me. Shit. I'm smiling. Damn it. I don't smile in these situations.

"I'm not going to untie you until we get to do it

again," she says smugly.

"You think you're that great at knots?" I ask her.

She sits back, folding her arms across those beautiful breasts. I can already feel myself coming back into action. "Name what they are," she says.

I glance up at the ties. I have no idea. "Timber hitch?" I ask.

She bursts out with a laugh. "Hardly. Try again."

"I think you're having too much fun," I say.

"I think I got you." She smacks her palm against my chest.

"Do you now?" I tense my chest muscles. "What about this?" I slide my wrists and the sash to the side of the frame I've already identified as having a weaker joint. With one quick jerk, the rod I'm tied to breaks away from the vertical bar. I slide the knots off the end and before Mia can fully react, bring my tied wrists behind her head.

In less than a second, I have her below me, her head cradled against my knots.

"I underestimated you," she says.

"Most people do," I tell her, and surprise her again when I plunge back into her body.

21

MIA

When I wake up a few hours later, Jax is standing at the window, looking out. He's naked still, and I take a moment to admire all of him. The light from the device delineates the muscles on his chest and the indentations of his abs.

I drop a little lower and feel a blush come over me. He's perfectly trimmed down there, and I remember what it was like with him hovering over me, erect and ready.

I take a little assessment of my body. Lots of

aches. My wrists hurt, probably from where that Klaus guy tied me. And down below, a sweet sort of swollen pulsing throb.

Jax notices I'm awake. "You feeling okay?" he asks. His voice isn't exactly tender, but he's asking, so I'll take it.

"I'm all right." I pull the sheet up to my neck, feeling inexplicably shy.

"I'm trying to decide if we'll wait for dawn to leave." He looks out the window again.

"Where are we going?"

Jax's fist tightens against his bicep, the only outward sign of any emotion. "Back to your house."

I jump from the bed, not caring that I'm naked. "You can't take me home again!"

Jax appraises my body and I flush with heat. "I'm not going to leave you there, Mia. Obviously if Klaus found you, my attachment to you is already known. You're safer with me."

Attachment? I hum inside at the word. Jax cares? And people know it?

Suddenly everything makes sense. Jax knew he couldn't leave me alone anymore. I glance down at my skin, flushed pink in places where his beard roughed it up. That's why he was willing to do this with me when he wasn't before.

I try to keep my voice steady, like he hasn't just rocked my world.

"Do you think Klaus is still there? I'm not sure my rope ties were *that* good," I say. It's been all night. Surely he's gotten free.

"He's not," Jax says. When he turns around to face me, I can see that my jumping from the bed has affected him. "Sam reports that all the monitors there show no activity."

"Are they coming here?" I'm torn between that hot erection and getting dressed before Jax's friends find us in yet another compromising position.

"No. They have their regular Vigilante duties to attend to, lest their assistance to me is discovered." He starts walking toward me.

My body responds with every step. The aches are erased in an instant as soon as my blood starts pumping. "So we're in no hurry?" I ask.

He lifts me up into his arms and covers the rest of the distance to the bed. "Not that much of one."

22

JAX

While Mia showers, I ball up the sheets and drop several large bills on top. I don't really want to deal with an innkeeper.

I spread out the stolen tech Mia took from Klaus. I don't expect that we will go much longer without intercepting him, and possibly Jovana. He's going to know I will come after him. The fact that he visited Mia alone is puzzling. From her account, he was fishing for information. No doubt he is as flummoxed as I am about her lack of data in the

Vigilante network.

The onyx ring she was wearing is on the floor by the bed. I pick it up. It's a curious piece, oval, and way too big for her fingers. I remember spotting it in the stash at her house that first night and slipping it on my finger to see if it had some special feature I didn't know about. By all appearances, it is just a ring. Maybe it made it into the Vigilante boxes by mistake. I drop it in the pile.

Mia comes out, still in the pajamas. She's all shy, eyes cast to the floor, plucking at her pajama shirt. She holds up the pair of men's shoes. "I forgot about these. Are they going to catch us now?"

She seems so frightened and lost that I want to comfort her. I force myself to smile instead. "Only trainees have trackers in their shoes," I say.

Her face shows so much relief that I laugh, a genuine one this time. "We'll stop somewhere that I can pick up an outfit for you," I tell her.

"We're going to my house, right?" she asks. "I can get my own things there."

I'm not sure how much to warn her about what's ahead. Even though the shoes aren't tracked and the car is wiped of Klaus, if he and Jovana have any sense, they will see our next move.

I don't care that they will lay a trap for us at Mia's house. I don't care that they will predict our arrival.

I just want my hands on both of them.

"Will you kill them?" Mia asks, so softly that I can barely make out her words.

"Who? Klaus and Jovana?"

"Is that her name? Jovana? Your old girlfriend?"

It sounds so quaint when she says it. Girlfriend.

"Yes, that's her name. And no, I won't necessarily kill them. But when you're in combat, you do what you have to do."

She puts Klaus's shoes back on, and we walk out to the car. "We're going to move the car I drove into town with to a secure location," I tell her.

"I could drive it back for you," she says.

"It's better if we stash it somewhere that we can access it."

Her head drops again. I guess she's expecting me to say something about last night, to act a certain way. But I don't do that. I'm not trying to start a relationship with her. There's no way that can work. I'm a fugitive, and this situation I'm in goes all the way to the top.

There's no way this can end well.

So I just walk out to the car and let her follow. We ride in silence through the community. When we've moved the stolen Vigilante car, I head out on the highway. I scan our route for law enforcement and impediments.

When all seems clear enough, I inject the accelerant, pleased at the powerful rumble of my own car as we shoot down the highway at four hundred miles per hour. For a short while, it's almost as if the terrible last year never happened.

Mia sits in silence, looking out the window at the blaze of passing trees and houses. "Life in the fast lane," she says softly.

"Surely makes you lose your mind," I add.

She watches me with those big green eyes. It's another moment that I could say something comforting about what happened between us. But I don't do it. I focus back on the road.

When we're about a mile from Mia's house, I tell her, "I'd feel better if you let me drop you off a good distance away. There will be traps set."

"No!" she insists. "It's my house. I know it better than anyone."

"I can't put you in that danger," I say, gripping

the steering wheel.

"The danger came to me!" Her voice is high and firm. "You won't keep me out of my own home!"

"It's a safe house, Mia. Full of traps and monitors and equipment stashes."

"I know!" she says. "I found the one under the pantry." Her voice gets quiet. "It had guns in it."

"See, that's what I'm talking about." The pine trees whiz by.

"What?" she asks.

"If you can't even look at a gun, how are you ever going to use one?"

We approach her drive. It's empty. Not even her old Ford is there. "Where is your car?" I ask.

"Up the road. Where I found this one."

I pass her house, then turn on the same dirt road I used when I parked in the field behind her property on that first night.

"I'm going to cross the fields and approach the house. You have to stay in the car. I will lock you in."

"You will not!"

"Mia, taking you with me puts me in great danger. I have to think about protecting you as well as myself."

This gets to her. She stares out the window.

"We'll talk the whole time." I park beside a big roll of hay and open the console between us, where I stashed the most essential of my gear. "Here's a secure videocam. You can see what I'm doing and we can talk the whole time."

It's a terrible idea, but I have already learned to hate disappointing her.

This is why I don't do relationships. It interferes with the job.

She takes the video chat device.

"Press this to see me." I punch a button on the top of the cam. The roof of the car shows up on the display.

"Okay," she says quietly.

I know I should do something comforting, so I lean over and kiss her. It's a mistake, because once I start, I don't want to stop. My protectiveness surges as she clutches at my shoulders.

"I'll be right back," I finally say.

She touches her lips. "You'll let me know when it's safe for me to come in?"

"I will."

The quiet surrounds me as I step from the car.

Country life. A rabbit or some ground rodent darts through the grass. Amazing what you can hear out here.

I reach for the bag I packed. “I’ll be on the chat,” I say to Mia, then close the door and secure it.

The house is about three hundred yards away. I pull out a monitor to use when I’m scanning the house. I no more power it up when it starts going off. Six traps in the field.

Interesting. They went all out on this one.

I don’t bother to diffuse these, but go around them. They are basic land mines. But another reason for Mia not to leave the car. I pick up the video chat.

“Mia, there are six land mines in your field. Don’t get out of the car.”

Her face shifts to panic. “Really?”

“Klaus is a real peach,” I say.

She looks out the windshield. I turn back to the car, but naturally I can’t see her with the false screens showing an empty car. Still, I know she’s there. She’s sensible and smart. She won’t get out of the car now.

I pass close to one of the mines, so I go ahead and bend down to disarm it. There’s nothing special about the tech they are using here. It’s almost as if they don't have access to anything that isn't standard issue.

With Sutherland in on their game, I would expect better.

When I'm about fifty yards from the house, I start to see some of the traps inside. Looks to be three. Kitchen, hallway, her bedroom.

There's nobody in the house, not as far as my sensors can see. They could be cloaked, though, and they could be completely still. When I get in a room, I can look for carbon dioxide emissions. I'm not especially worried about a personal attack, though. Klaus is a security guy, and Jovana, well, I overpowered her many times, in bed and out of it.

I glance at the screen on the video, a pinch of guilt nagging at me just for thinking it. Mia is staring straight into the screen, anxious and silent.

"It's going fine," I tell her.

She nods but doesn't look any more relaxed.

I step onto the porch. The kitchen trap is an air pressure bomb, designed to go off when I open the door. The cool air moving inside triggers it. I move to the kitchen window and cut a neat circle in the pane over the lock.

I inch the window up gradually, allowing the

room to adjust in temperature and barometric pressure. Then I carefully pop the locks on the door. There are a half dozen, but I opened them that first night. For a safe house, it is only marginally secure.

I ease open the door, avoiding that push of air that happens when you enter quickly. They probably expected I would come in with guns blazing. Maybe they thought I wouldn't have any tech to identify their traps.

The bomb is just inside the door. It's a simple matter now of walking up to it and shutting off the sensor. Now I can take it if I want it for myself. I pick it up and set it on the counter.

The pantry door is open and I have to smile when I see the shattered floor that reveals the metal hatch. That's no Vigilante job. Mia must have managed to get it open. I turn my camera to show it. "Is this your work?" I ask her.

She nods and gives half a smile.

"Subtle," I say.

This gets more of a reaction.

"Just two more to go," I say.

The hallway bomb is a motion-sensor trigger. Maybe they hoped Mia herself would rush to her room. The thought of them hurting or killing her makes my blood start to pound.

It's a smallish bomb, designed to maim someone at close range. "I'm just going to set this one off," I tell Mia. "Don't panic if you hear it fire."

She nods.

I glance around the kitchen and spot a basket of oranges on the counter. I pick one up and head to the door to the hall. With a swift motion, I set the orange rolling down the hall and back away.

The POP of the bomb rings in my ears. I check the scanner. It's the only one, and done. I glance at my handiwork. The wallpaper is scarred near the blast, and the floor is a little damaged. But overall, not too bad.

Just the one near her bedroom to go.

I approach the closed door with caution. They've set up something my scanner can't quite identify. But the previous blast would have set off anything triggered by motion, sound, or pressure. So it's something else.

Her door is tied like a gift with a large blue and yellow knot in the center.

"They've tied us a puzzle," I say to Mia. I turn the video so she can see. "It's a blood knot."

"What's the trap?" she asks.

"I don't know. I assume if I untie it, it will blow."

"Must be a joke since Klaus was probably not happy I tied him up."

It actually sounds like something Jovana would do, but I don't tell Mia that.

I scan the door. There's another explosive on the other side, a big one. It could theoretically take out half the house.

"Looks like if I put too much pressure on the knot, it will blow," I say.

"Just walk away," Mia says.

"I'll diffuse it," I tell her. "I just have to untie it without creating any additional tautness in the line."

"Let me see it closer," she says.

"It's simple," I say. "A normal blood knot linking to different-colored ropes." I point to the blue and yellow parts. "It's like in the barn. I just have to work into the knot instead of away."

"A blood knot is tightened by pulling on the opposite lines," she says. "So sure, you can push them toward each other to undo it."

"Not a problem," I say and slip the video in the pocket. "I'll be back out in just a few minutes, and I can show you how to disarm a land mine."

"Show me that knot again," she says, but I don't pull the camera out of my pocket.

"It'll just take a second," I say. Carefully, I push the loose ends toward the center of the knot to give it some play.

This will be a cinch.

23

MIA

The darkness when Jax puts the camera away fills me with dread.

Such a strange choice of knot. A blood knot. That's a difficult one to tie on a door. You need access to both ends, and if it's around an object, it's hard to do. A hitch would have made more sense.

I picture the knot in my mind, the blue and the yellow. It appears to be a classic blood knot, the yellow rope going into the blue coil, and the blue rope going into the yellow.

But something about it feels wrong. I hold the camera and fuss a second with the settings. Yes, it's like the old DVRs. I can pause it and rewind to view the recording.

And I see it. What bothered me. The yellow and blue lines going into the coils are slightly thicker than the coil. It's not the same rope.

He's wrong. That's not a blood knot at all.

It's a trick.

"Jax! Wait! Don't pull on it!" I yell into the phone.

But it's too late.

The windows blow out as an explosion rocks the house.

You've reached the end of Vigilante's Lover #2!

Another cliffie! I know! Sorry!

Come ~~scream~~ talk about the cliffhangers
on Facebook with Annie's Vigilantes:

www.facebook.com/groups/anniesvigilantes

Join the mail list to make sure
you don't miss a release!

www.anniewinters.com

Annie has continued her grand tradition of killer endings that began with her work as JJ Knight. Fans don't call her the Queen of Cliffhangers for nothing!

Annie and Tony are modeling *Vigilante* after the structure of television suspense series. We release very quickly so you don't have long to wait!

www.ingramcontent.com/pod-product-compliance
Lightning Source LLC
Chambersburg PA
CBHW021035130626
46552CB00005B/1849
9781938150388